Julian

THE STANTON PACK BOOK 3

KATHI S. BARTON

This is a work of fiction. Names, characters, places, and incidents are products of the author's imagination or are used fictitiously and are not to be construed as real. Any resemblance to actual events, locations, organizations, or persons, living or dead, is entirely coincidental.

World Castle Publishing, LLC
Pensacola, Florida
Copyright © Kathi S. Barton 2018
Paperback ISBN: 9798891263895
eBook ISBN: 9781629899107
First Edition World Castle Publishing, LLC, March 19, 2018
http://www.worldcastlepublishing.com
Licensing Notes
Cover: Karen Fuller
Editor: Maxine Bringenberg

Table of Contents

Chapter 1

Julian was enjoying his breakfast at the little diner when the man walked in. There was something about him that made Julian want to pull out his gun and blow his head off. No reason that he could see right now for such a violent reaction, but he hated the man on sight. Taking his handgun out of his pocket, he laid it on the seat next to him. There wasn't a safety, but had there been one, he would have taken it off as well. Something—something very bad was surrounding this man.

"I'm looking for Tess O'Rourke, she's a friend of my son's. She's a doctor of some kind." Sally told him she didn't know her but did know an Ericson with the same last name. The man's voice was off too. Like he was trying his best to project a woman's voice. Odd, even to him. "Yeah, that's her grandddad. Where is he?"

"I'm sorry, but I don't know you from Adam, and I'm not going to tell you that." She went by him with a pot of coffee in her hand. When he was close enough to touch her, Sally, a wolf shifter, stepped back when he grabbed her. "You touch me without my permission and they'll be picking up pieces of you out of this place for the next fifty years."

She poured the coffee for the table next to Julian's, then came to him. He could tell that she was upset, but all he did was lay his gun on the table. For that reason alone, he was sure, she looked relieved. Saying nothing and going back to the counter, she asked the man if he wanted anything to eat.

"I already told you want I wanted. Now, either call him up or send some kid to find him, but you're to do as you're told." Sally cocked her brow at him. "You heard me. I'm not in the habit of repeating myself to people. Get him or face me."

Finished with his meal now that this ass had interrupted it, Julian wiped his mouth with his napkin, picked up his gun, and put it to the back of the man's head when he stood up. Julian winked at Sally before speaking.

"Sally, honey, if you'd be so kind as to call the police, I'd surely appreciate it. If I have to kill this man for simply being a rude fucktard, then I want them here to make sure that I did it by the law." The man started to lunge, to where he had no idea, but Julian popped him hard in the back of the head and the man fell like he'd had strings cut that were holding him up. "Now look what you made me do. Sally, tell them we're going to need the wagon too. I hurt him."

When the police arrived, not really in any kind of hurry since Sally had told them it was Julian, they took one look at the man on the floor and laughed. Apparently, he'd been all over town ordering people to do his bidding.

"Mr. Merkel, he's none too happy with him either. I guess when he was busy with another customer, this guy here swiped his hand over the counter, breaking his wife's best glass of tea. The glass, not the tea." Julian laughed with them. "Have you ever had her tea? Good God oh mighty, don't, if you haven't. It's sweet enough that I'm betting she uses five pounds of sugar in it to make it that sweet."

The medics brought the man around, and after a few minutes he finally stood. But when he looked around, trying, no doubt, to figure out who had hit him, his gaze settled on the man at the table, one of the nicest men in town. He was also Julian's father.

"You touch him, and it will be over before you can get all your fingers wrapped around him." The man looked at Julian, then at his dad. "He didn't hit you. Not that he might not have, but I did it. For being an ass. In this town, we don't order people around, nor do we suggest they fetch and do as told for an asshole."

"Julian, behave." He told his mom he was sorry, but he didn't take his eyes off the man. "Come sit with us and let the police handle this one. Perry is doing a very good job as our new sheriff. That man there is unbalanced."

"Listen here, bitch—"

He got no further because Julian's sweet little mother got up and punched the stranger in the face. Then she sat down and picked up her menu.

"I think I'm going to have the eggs and bacon today, Denny. Julian, I said come away from there before you have to hurt that man again." She laid her menu down and smiled at him. "I do not usually resort to violence, but he drove me

7

to it. Now, what are you having, Denny?"

Julian might not have ever believed it if he'd not seen it for himself. His mom was taking some self-defense training from Allie, and it seemed to be paying off. Julian had thought his mom was scary before; now she was simply terrifying. He sat back down as the man, still the only thing he knew him by, was taken out.

"We can't arrest him for being a dick—pardon, Mrs. Stanton—being a bad-mouthed man, but we've told him to move on. I don't think he will." Julian told Perry, his brother-in-law, that he didn't believe he would either. "We'll just keep an eye out for him. You'll help us out, won't you, Jules?"

Lately, just in the last couple of weeks, he'd been having his name shortened. He didn't hate it as much as Brayden did; he actually thought it was nice. Friendly. As he drank a nice cup of tea with his parents, who had entered the diner when the man was out, he asked them if there was a Tess around.

"Oh yes. I think that's her name. She's the granddaughter to my buddy, Ericson O'Rourke. He's going to be working on that vet, Kendal Wayne, that came in with the bullet in his head. Why no one tried to remove it when he was hurt is beyond me, but he'll be operated on in the morning, I guess."

Julian nodded and sipped his tea while his mom took up where Dad had left off.

"The young woman, Kendal Wayne's wife Sandra, she's been helping out at the veteran's office. I've never seen anyone so organized before. When the donations started coming in, she had them all in the proper order in no time. So, we put her in charge of procurement. I thought it was a nice title. And she's being paid." Julian said that was good. "But this man, what does he have to do with Tess?"

"Don't know. I guess, according to Perry, that he's been all over town asking for her—well, you heard him—demanding her to come to him. I don't know what his deal was." Mom told him that she wasn't married. "Don't set me up. I have enough going on right now without trying to untangle myself from a woman that you think is pretty."

"I've never met her yet, as a matter of fact, but I was saying she wasn't married because whoever this man is, he's not her husband." He told her he was sorry. "But would it hurt you to go to see her to see if she is your mate? I heard that she's as sweet as pie, too."

"Mom." Mom laughed when Dad did. "I sign on my house in the morning. Also, since you did ask me, the furniture comes with it. I don't know what I'm going to do with all of it, but for the most part, I'm going to keep it. Maybe sort of swap it out for something that I find while keeping the house looked lived in." Julian had an apartment too, one that he'd never released when he'd been working. For some reason, he didn't want to let it go. There might be a good reason for him keeping it someday. "Mom, do you think that Dane or Allie would want the baby stuff that was left behind? There is a lot of it. Girl stuff."

"I don't know, you'd have to ask them. But I think that Allie and her parents are having a good time getting the nursery ready for the baby. And Dane will more than likely hurt you if you suggest that she needs pink in her baby's room." He laughed with his dad, saying that camo would be better for any child born to Dane and Brayden. "Oh good heavens, you don't really think that's what she's doing, do you? Camo? Oh my."

"I'll just leave it then. It's not like it's bothering me." But it was. He had no idea why, but he had the most incredible urge to not just fill the nursery, but the house too. Telling his mom and dad he had to go, he left them there.

The streets were cleaned of the early morning snow now, but he didn't care. There was a feeling of hope in the air too. The new year was here, the stores were getting ready for spring, and he had an interview with the police force in the next town over. It would be a good drive, about forty minutes, but he thought it was better than just sitting around the house and being bored.

His cell phone was ringing when he got into his truck. Julian was startled to hear screams first, then shots fired. Perry asked him to meet him at the local hotel, and he was to come hot and ready.

"Fucking hurry."

He did, and when he pulled up in front of the place, he saw three people that he didn't know, as well as child services. Not having any idea what he was walking in on, he decided that safe was better than sorry. Taking his gun out, he approached the man from the diner.

"What the fuck are you doing now? I thought we had this conversation not ten minutes ago." The man turned and swung, and Julian dodged it. The guy went down, and Julian put his boot on his back, glad to see that he'd landed in some mud. "Now, this is what you're going to do. Tell me what the fuck is wrong with you?"

"She's not supposed to have that kid. No kids, no kids, no kids. I told her she didn't need them." Not sure who he was talking about, he looked at Betty Cobb, the town social worker. The man continued speaking. "Tess is a terrible mom; she's a whore that doesn't need to have children. I've seen her beating that baby and leaving it out in the cold. Just let me have it and I'll make sure that it's taken care of."

Whatever the man meant by his statement, it made Julian feel sick to his stomach. A combination of the woman-like voice and the way he said "take care of it" made his skin crawl too. Julian would rather die than to give that kid over to this person. He looked at Betty.

"The baby is fine. But we've taken her to the hospital with her mom." He asked if she was all right. "Yes, but the baby is a little upset, if you can imagine. No indication of any marks on her, and she's a chubby little thing too. Cute as a button."

"He do anything to hurt them?" Betty told him that Ruby, the baby's name, had a cold, but that they were checking her out because of what he'd said. "And what is he doing here? Father? Brother?"

"Nuisance." Julian looked at the older gentleman when the idiot under his foot struggled to get away. Julian just pressed him harder into the mud until he was gasping. "He's not any relation to us, but he has it in his head that he needs to have the baby for some reason. I know this man; this isn't like him at all. Usually he's so quiet and timid. And he doesn't want my Tess, just her baby. Like I said, I don't know what's come over him. This isn't him. Oh, by the way, my name is Ericson O'Rourke. You have to be related to Denny."

"His son. Julian Stanton, third son to them. And you're the doctor that came here to operate on Kendal." He said that he was. "Kendal is a good man, doesn't deserve this. I surely hope you can do some good for him."

"I will give it my best, but before you drown Dexter, let him up."

Jules grinned at Perry when he finally showed up.

"I had to escort Ms. O'Rourke. She's pretty upset too."

After Dexter Jorden was taken in, Julian asked Perry if he needed him for anything else. Perry said the same thing he always did, to come and work for him. He told him again that it wasn't in the cards. Just as he was leaving his parents showed up, and he hung with them to figure out what the guy's deal was that was after this Tess person.

~~~

Tess watched her little girl as the nurse examined her. Ruby had a bruise on her right shoulder, but otherwise was all right. Dexter was off the deep end, and she didn't have any idea what to do about him. When the doctor invited her to come into his office, she asked if she could pick up Ruby and was told she could. Holding her little girl tightly, she handed her the binky that she had and watched her little eyes drift closed. It really had been a long day, and it wasn't even ten in the morning yet.

"She's had a rough day, I think." She told Doctor Colton that she had. "I'm sorry. I'm Doc Stanton. My first name is Colton. You're Tess O'Rourke, the surgeon we've heard so much about lately."

"I am. My granddad is the one that was called in, but word travels fast. I guess that happens in a small town. You're related to the man that called my granddad, then." He said that he was his son. "I see. Is my little girl going to be all right? I mean, he grabbed her pretty hard when he tried to take her from me."

"Yes, she's just fine. And so you're aware, I'm only here helping out — I'm actually a retiring psychologist. I work here when they're short of staff or need a break." She thanked him for coming in. "My pleasure. I had no idea that Ericson had a great granddaughter, much less a granddaughter."

"I'm his only relative, and since I'm not working at the moment, I decided to come along with him. Ruby likes to travel too. See things like snow. I had no idea there would be nothing left of it already." He told her it was Ohio — tomorrow it might be in the seventies or the teens. "I've heard that before, I think. Sally at the diner told us."

"Yes, she's good on sayings. And talking." They both laughed. "You can take Ruby home with you if you'd like. On one condition."

Her body stiffened. "I might have a child, Dr. Stanton, but I'm not easy." He laughed, and she felt her temper flare up hotter. "You would be well enough to just leave me alone."

"Feel better?" She wasn't sure what he meant and asked him. "I'm not that other man. I was just asking you if you'd like to have dinner with me, at my parents' house, with them there. I have my own home, but I know that your granddad is going to be there, and I didn't hear that you would."

"I wasn't invited." Her temper now was turned onto herself. "I'm sorry. I've had a rough few months too. No, Ruby and I are trying to lay low with Dexter around here now. I don't know what's come over him lately. He used to be such a loving, kind man. But if he keeps this up, we might have to take off again. I don't want to, but I don't want my daughter be hurt by him. He's not usually so violent."

13

"Yes, he is. How many ribs do you have broken right now." She didn't say anything. "You have two, I would say, on your left, more on the right. You're breathing hard and shallow. And you carry the baby on the less pained side. Also, there is a ligature mark on your neck. Most might not see it, but I'm paid to. Where are the rest of them? When he hits you, he's usually so careful, isn't he? This man Dexter or your husband do that?"

"I don't have a husband, as you well know. But yes, it's Dexter. He is still mourning the death of his mom. I don't know why he'd be like this—they weren't close. Actually, I never liked her at all, even when we were children. But I think it's affected him somehow and he's acting out." He asked her how long it had been. "Let me see. Ruby is six months old, and it was about eight months before that, so I'd say a year and a half. No more than that."

She watched as he looked at her daughter. "She's not his." The tears started to flow and before she knew it, not only was she sitting down, but was doing so in a very nice office too. Ruby was gone from her arms, and she had a box of tissues as she told him everything.

"Dexter told me that he didn't want me to have a baby that day. I was just a little over nine weeks pregnant. Kenneth and I, we weren't in love, but he was security for me at work. So men would stop hitting on me. And I was security for his place of work as well. Kenneth had a lover and we were all going to live together. But they wanted a child, so they helped me with my student loans and I helped by being their surrogate. Then one day after I'd heard that his mom was dead, Dexter came at me, screaming at me to get rid of it. He

14

kept saying no kids, over and over. He must have hit me." Colton asked her if she'd been hurt by it. "No. Just a nasty bump to the head, but it knocked me out. They told me when I woke that Kenneth was gone. We'd not gotten married yet, and now I have Ruby, which I wouldn't change for all the money in the world. But I do miss him and Daniel."

"There's more too, isn't there? Tell me, Tess, so that I can help you." She didn't want his help, but after today, knew that she was going to need it. "What did he do recently that has you so terrified?"

"I've lost my job because of him. A couple of weeks before I did, he would come to my office and would harass me. Once, when I was in surgery, he hurt three of the staff to get to me, then had to be arrested when he tried to enter the operating room." Colton said nothing, but now that the dam was opened, she couldn't stop the flow of words. "I have nothing. He's taken all my cash somehow, and then when I go to the police, there isn't any proof that he took it. Nothing. I've changed banks and cards. Nothing seems to stop him. I've been beaten so many times that I can't tell where a new bruise begins and the old one ends. I've lost everything since he's been like this. My car, my job, my reputation. Thankfully he never bothers Granddad or me when I'm with him. But he's obsessed with Ruby and her going with him. And for some reason, I think he means to hurt her."

"You're a surgeon, like your granddad." She nodded, telling him that she'd only just gotten her license to practice here. "In this hospital? You're going to move here?"

"Granddad wants to, but now, with this, I don't think I should. I mean, he could, and Dexter might hurt him to get to

15

me. And I can't have him hurt the only man that I love." He looked at her sharply. "Yes, Kenneth and I did like each other like friends, and I liked his partner, Daniel, one too, but.... Kenneth was...his parents were pressuring him to marry a woman. But I knew from the very beginning that we weren't suited. Yes, I liked him, very much. We did create a child together too, by artificial insemination, but we never really loved like a man and woman do. We both knew that going in."

"All right. This helps me a great deal." She asked him how. "Well, for starters, you're going to have dinner at my family home tonight. Then we're going to get you out of the hotel. There isn't enough protection there. Not to mention, he might hurt others in trying to get to you. Which he won't again."

"And how do you think you're going to do that? He's already been released. And in the event that you didn't notice, Dexter doesn't seem to get into trouble for shit that he does." Ruby had just started crawling, and instead of going to her, she crawled to Colton. "That's a first."

"Do you believe in shifters?" Yes, she told him, he was a cougar, all his family was. "Okay, yes, your granddad would have told you. I'm sorry. But that makes it easier for me to tell you that so long as you're around here, you'll be safe. We protect family, and since you're a friend of my dad's, then you're family."

"I don't think it works that way." He, much to the delight of her daughter, bounced Ruby on his knee. When she placed her head on his shoulder again to take a longer nap, she assumed, he laid her back in the crook of his arms and held her. "You're very good with babies."

"My sisters-in-law are both breeding, so I've been practicing. I can even change a poopie diaper, fill a bottle with one hand, and feed a rambunctious two-year-old." He kissed Ruby on the forehead before rocking her back and forth. "I'll have one of my brothers come by later and get you packed with the rest of your things, if that's all right. I've spoken to my parents, and since your granddad is helping out, then they'd love for the three of you to stay with them. Mom needs practice too, she said. She's not held a little girl for years."

As he was ready to go when she was, he gave her a lift to the hotel. The snow had begun to fall again, and she was afraid for Ruby. The little girl's car seat was at the hotel, so she held her tightly as they took the slickest roads she'd ever been on. At least since living in Florida most of her life.

Colton drove slowly but she was still afraid. Even as they made it there in one piece, she didn't want to leave again. But Colton insisted that they come to his parents' for dinner, and she couldn't turn him down again. He'd been a nice man to her — the first nice man in a long time, it seemed.

Gathering what she would need to perhaps stay all night at a strange home, Colton's phone rang when she was taking him the car seat. While he was putting the cheap thing into his truck, the back split open and it simply fell apart. She looked at him as he threw it in the back of his truck and smiled at her. It was too much. Dropping to sit in the snow, she started crying again.

"Come on now, get up before you get a cold where you can't take medication. I have no idea what that means, but my grandma used to say that to me all the time. Asses can't get colds, and cougars don't catch them anyway." He helped her inside and handed her a box of tissues. "My mom is coming with my brother. And they're picking up a car seat for Ruby. And if you tell me no, I'm going to make you deal with my mom. She's not one to mess with."

"Everything I have is cheap, or second hand and cheap." She stopped crying enough to check on Ruby. "This child can sleep through anything. I swear, I wish I could have one nap as good as she does."

"You're not very good at changing the subject, which is all right, but I have to go to the hospital for a psych evaluation. That's why my mom is coming." Again, she tried to tell him she'd just stay there. "No, you won't. If you don't agree, now that my mom is coming, she's going to bully you into coming anyway. And Julian, my brother, he's not having such a good day either, and a hug from Ruby will be just the thing for him. He's the one that had Dexter arrested today."

"Then he's great in my book. Probably could be king for the day too." They were laughing when he went to the door with her. She smiled when he told her to lock up. "Yes, Daddy, and I won't answer the phone until it rings once, then you call back."

Laughing, he thanked her. As he moved out the door, Colton turned back to look at her once again. There was a strange look on his face and she nearly asked him what was wrong, but he was gone before she could. Strange, but a nice man. She locked the door and went to check again on Ruby. She, of course, was sound asleep.

Chapter 2

Julian knew less about car seats than he did about making a pretty bouquet of flowers. So, he pulled out his phone and started looking them up. Cost didn't matter, Colton told him, just get the best one. Julian knew that cost didn't always factor in on how well things worked.

Mom found him about ten minutes later with a cart load of things. Pink seemed to be the color of choice, but he could also see greens and reds. He laughed when she asked him about diaper bags.

"I thought he said just to get her a car seat that was worthy of his friend." Mom smiled at him. "I'm going to get this one. Out of four thousand reviews, it has four and a half stars. I guess that's the best we're going to get. And I so love that you've gotten pink too."

"You have all those things at your house that are pink as well. I thought maybe when she gets settled, you'd take them to her." Julian wanted to tell her no, but he nodded at his mom as they made their way to the front. "And honey, if you don't mind, you'll have to go get her yourself. Your dad needs me to help him in the clinic. One of the Rogers' children has broken his arm."

"I'll look into that too." She thanked him. "All right. Where do you want me to drop you off?"

She told him Dad was coming. "And when you bring her over, please try not to scare her." He asked why she'd say that. "Because you carry a gun. That's enough to scare most people. Just try to be super nice to her. I guess having that young man around terrorizing her is a little much on anyone."

When she left him, he went to the baby department again and picked up diapers. Dane said that kids always needed diapers. Reading the boxes, he didn't have a clue, so he got the size for the months old he'd been told. Then, for added security, he got one size larger and one smaller. Just to be safe, he told himself. And while walking by the little shoes, he picked up a pair of little boots that looked like his. Smiling, he went to the cash register.

Four hundred and eighty-four dollars later, he was reading the instructions on how to put the car seat in his truck. Several times after starting over he was sure that it had been made by some mad man in order to rid the population of second children being born. It was that, or he was going to have to sell his truck to get rid of the thing. Giving up, he just put it in the back and went to the apartment complex.

Julian loved the old hotel, but his brother was right; there just weren't enough safety measures in place for when someone was in trouble. Going up the elevator with several people, he felt good about people asking him about the bags.

He wanted to tell them that he had a new daughter but knew that most of the people knew his parents and would be upset at the fib. Knocking at the door, he told the woman on the other side what his name was and who had sent him. The screaming child had his cat stirring badly.

"She is upset." He told her he could see that when the woman shoved the baby at him and walked out of the room. "I didn't hurt her. I was just taking a shower and I didn't hear her. Then when I didn't come right away, I guess she got more upset, and then more so, and now she hates me."

"You're over doing it a little." The baby calmed down when he spoke. "She's okay now if you want to finish your shower. You still have shampoo on your—"

"I know that. Why is it she is quiet for you?" He shrugged and handed the baby one of the many toys that his mom had purchased. "Where did that come from? It's adorable."

"My mom. She went with me to get the car seat. Which I haven't the slightest clue how to put in. You'd think with a PhD I could put it in without cursing." She smiled, and Julian smiled back. "You're very pretty. I'm sure you know that."

"I'm standing here in a towel with wet hair, and shampoo, as you so rudely pointed out, still in my hair. I have to finish shaving my legs, and.... Why am I telling you this?" He said he didn't know but she could go on. "No, I think I'll stop while I can. If you really don't mind holding her, I'll only be a few more minutes."

"Take your time. My mom said we have a couple of hours before dinner. Her and Dad are setting the arm of a little boy." Julian took the baby to the couch and laid her on it. She was staring at him like he was going to do tricks, so he stuck his

21

tongue out at her. When her lower lip started to quiver, he quickly picked her up and spoke to her. "No, come on now. Don't cry for me. I was just playing. I don't know much about little girls."

He could smell her diaper. And as much as he didn't want to get into changing a nasty one, he knew that he'd not like that either. Taking her to the little bedroom where they'd come from, he looked at what he might need.

"I'm hoping that you appreciate this." He grabbed two diapers, glad that he'd gotten one box the right size, and the wipe things, and a little bag that people with dogs took on trails to clean up. "If this is up your back, like I've heard some babies do, then you're on your own, kid."

The diaper wasn't that bad, but the smell was nasty. He started talking to her just to make himself feel better about disrobing a child that he didn't know. She sure was a pretty little girl, and he started there.

"I guess you look like your momma, huh? Good thing, I guess. Looking like someone like me means you won't ever get a date, much less a husband. I'm ugly. Well, not ugly, but I don't look like a pretty little girl, now do I?" He got the diaper off her and then wiped her clean, using about a dozen of the wet things. "No powder, kid. I couldn't find it. There was some creamy stuff in a tube, but I don't think I know you well enough to go touching your privates with that stuff. What do you think?"

"I think you're very handy to have around." He smiled up at Tess when she entered the bedroom with him. "I'm so sorry. I don't usually freak out, but it's been a day from heck."

"Yeah, mine too. My mom bought her a lot of little girly

things. I brought them in with me. I think I might have dropped them when you gave me the baby. What's her name, by the way?" She told him. "Ruby. I love that. She looks like a little gem too. And all this hair. I saw some hair things in the bags too."

While she was getting the bags, he was thinking about the clothing that he'd seen on the conveyor belt. Julian thought with her coloring, the little red dress with tights might be the ticket. When her mom returned, she dumped everything on the bed and sat down with a flop. That was when he caught her scent.

"Christ." She looked at him. Julian wasn't sure what to say to her so he said nothing but held the baby a little too tightly and she fussed at him. "I'll just wait for you in there."

Putting Ruby back on the bed, he darted to the living room. Christ. Christ. Christ. His mate — she was his mate, and he had a house for them. Perfectly groomed for them. When she came out of the bedroom dressed, Tess handed him the baby again while she put on her shoes. Ruby had on the red dress and the little white tights with hearts on them. Also a ribbon in her hair.

"You're upset about something." He nodded, then shook his head. "In there, with Ruby, you seemed to be having fun. Then when I put the clothing on the bed, you freaked out. I need to know what I did. Was it the clothing? I can't, at least right at the moment, afford to pay you back for —"

"No, that's not it. Mom would have my head if I even thought of you paying her back. No, that's not it." He started to pace the room. "I'm a cougar. I'm sure you're aware of that."

"Yes. Your dad and my granddad are friends." He nodded, distracted by her legs sticking out of the bottom of her skirt. "Your name is Julian. Do you go by Jules?"

"Not usually, but then if you want to call me that, it's fine." How to tell her? "I bought a house a while back. I just moved in a couple of weeks ago. The couple got a divorce, and since they couldn't decide on who got what, the judge ordered it sold. I bought it from the auction house, as is."

She nodded. "I don't know you well, but you seem to be rambling. Is that your normal way to get around the bush?" He shook his head and told her he was nervous. "Nervous? From what I heard, today you took down Dexter. Not once but twice. I wish that I could have seen that."

"He hurt you and Ruby. That's going to be a problem for him now." She asked him why it would be one now. "You're my mate, Tess."

He let her think while he went to get Ruby. She was fussing, and while he had read someplace that you didn't pick them up when they fussed, he needed her more than she needed him. Picking her up in his arms, he spoke in low tones to her.

"You're going to be something, I'm betting. I wonder if you'll like me. Probably not. I'm not going to allow you to date until.... Well, never. I don't care what your mom says. I was a boy once, and I am not going to allow any one of them to touch you." A throat being cleared had him turning. "I'm nervous still."

"She's not going to date? How do you figure that'll work?" He said he didn't know anything about babies. "Yet she quiets when you hold her. And I'm thinking that she'll have you wrapped around her finger in no time. But that does not mean you will me."

"No, I didn't think so. I had hopes, but no, I didn't think so." She shook her head. "I'm going to take you both to my parents' house where we're going to have a nice meal, and then we can talk. Is that all right with you?"

"I'm not sure." He felt his cat stir when the baby fussed at him. "She doesn't normally trust others. I think it has to do with Dexter always trying to harm me."

"If he touches you again, he's dead." Tess only stared at him, then nodded. "You believe me?"

"Yes, I do. I've been around shifters before. Not cats, but mostly wolves. I saw a bear once as well, but that's not important. If I am your mate—" He told her that she was. "If I am your mate, then you'll be subjected to a lot of male scents on me. I'm a social person. I love to hug, and if you hurt my grandfather or my daughter while we're figuring this out, you'll be dead. Understand?"

"Yes. I understand." He kissed the baby on the fat cheek and then licked her throat. "If he hurts her or takes her, I want to be able to find her and him. Also you, if you'll allow it."

"Not yet." He understood. "All right. I have to gather a diaper bag up. And fill it. I didn't have one before your mom went shopping. Things have been extremely tight for me."

"Dexter?" She nodded as she picked up the pretty outfits and then folded them gently before putting them in the bag. "There's something else you should be aware of. The house, the one I was telling you about. It has a nursery in it. It was a little girl's nursery."

"Did anyone die in your house? I know you said that

they were divorced, but no one died there, correct?" He told her what he'd heard. "Oh. Yes, I can see why he'd not want the baby things after finding out the child wasn't his. Kind of selfish. Are you going to be like that? Treat her differently because she's not your child?"

"Never. As far as I'm concerned, she is my child, now and forever." He watched her face, and when she seemed to believe him, he helped her put the baby in the parka coat-like sack thingy. "What the hell is this thing? I swear to you, I'm selling my truck once we get that car seat in and we don't need it anymore. I might have to get something roomier I guess, too. You drive?"

"Yes. Why?" He just shrugged. "Why did you ask me if I drove or not? Don't do that, Jules. I can't have you doing things just because you think they're best for me or Ruby. While she might love you for it, I won't."

"I won't. But I was thinking you'd need a four-wheel drive car. The roads around here are shit—" Tess cleared her throat. "I guess I'd better clean up my act, huh?"

"I don't know what you should do, but cursing around my daughter is a no-no." Jules, as he figured he was going to be called by her, thought of not cursing around her daughter. He wanted to tell her that it was their daughter but knew better. She wouldn't like him until he could prove himself to her through the little girl.

After she showed him how to put the snowsuit—what she called the monster suit from He...Hades—on Ruby, he carried the bag out to the car and started it. Warming it up for his girls, he reached out to his dad. Dad would tell the world he had a mate, he didn't doubt that one bit.

~~~

Tess wasn't sure what to do about the man. He was polite, kind, and Ruby seemed to really like him. When she was fussy, all Tess had to do was hand her over to Jules and the two of them would bond. It was the strangest thing she'd ever seen.

"Would you come into the kitchen with me?" Nodding at Mrs. Stanton, she followed the women, Dane and Allie too, into the large kitchen. "Dane wanted to let you know about Dexter."

"Dexter? I thought you were having me in here to warn me off of Jules. And I have to tell you something. I'm not sure that I'd let you. He's a kind man. Courteous to everyone he meets. When I was putting the car seat in his truck, I scratched the paint and all he did was laugh. Laugh. What man laughs when a woman does that to his truck?" All three of them said Julian. "Oh. Well, I won't let you. Warn me off, I mean. I've.... Why did you call me in here?"

They all three laughed. She was so embarrassed that she laughed with them. "Dexter, honey; we called you in here because Dane has some information on your tormentor."

"Dexter passed his psych test today. Colton went to give it to him, and when he was finished, there was no reasonable explanation as to why he went off on you today." She said that he was mourning. "I don't think that's all of it. Did you know that at one time he had a girlfriend, Alma? We're still looking into that, but so far all we've been able to find out is that she's missing. Her parents are looking hard, but they don't suspect Dexter at all."

"Who do they suspect?" They looked at each other, then

at her. "Not me. I didn't do anything with her."

"I don't think they know anything just yet, but it might come back on you. I'd not worry about it. And in that, they've been feeding their local police force information, like how you have everything, and their little girl is out there without. We think that might be Dexter's reasoning for taking all that you have." She asked Dane what she thought. "Right now? Nothing. Accusing, beyond the information I have, isn't going to get us what we want. But if you're asking me if I think you had anything to do with her disappearance, then no, I don't. None of us do."

Tess sat down. There was such a feeling of relief that she didn't have it in her to be upright at the moment. When she put her head between her knees to catch herself a breath or two, the noises in the room changed and a pair of men's boots were suddenly in her sight.

"They call you in here?" Jules laughed and said that they had. "I'm not guilty of doing anything to Alma. Who names their child that?"

"I don't know. Who's Alma?" She told him what Dane had said to her. "Ah, well, she had some far-reaching hands. Do you feel better now? I'd like to kiss you."

Tess looked up at him and didn't know what to think about him. He was really charming and kind. And she had no idea why he made her feel like she could curl into his arms and never worry about herself or Ruby again.

"What is it about you that makes me want to let you take care of me?" He pulled out one of the chairs from the table and sat beside her. "You give me comfort by just being in the room. My daughter has never made me feel like I could just let her roam a house with strangers in it until you came along. And for that matter, Ruby doesn't like any man but my granddad. Yet she lets you not only hold her, but you can change her diaper, put her in a little outfit, and she says not a single thing."

"I'm a cougar. And before you dismiss that, let me explain. I'm a cat, someone that nurtures and loves. Also, within my DNA is this thing that compels me to care for my other half. But with you, I have to be honest with you, Tess, I think even without that little extra, I'd want to hold and take care of the two of you. You already own a part of my heart. Ruby has the other part." She asked him what he'd do if she said no to the kiss. "Then I'd ask again and again until you say yes. Or you kiss me. Shall we join the others?"

The man was going to drive her bonkers. He took her hand and she went with him to the living room. They were all gathered in small groups—if you could call men as large as these small. Even Dr. Stanton was a big man. And she'd bet that not one of them had an ounce of fat on them. When her granddad showed up, she felt balanced. And why that thought popped into her head, she didn't know.

Ruby started getting tired right before dinner. Tess told them to go ahead without her and asked for a room that she could nurse her in. She had wanted to sit alone and feed her baby, but when Jules asked if he could sit with her, she couldn't turn him down. When she had her daughter at her breast, he sat back in the other chair and watched her.

"You're making me feel uncomfortable." He smiled at her but said nothing. "When you smile like that, all I can think of is how you must have gotten your way as a little boy. I'm betting a great deal too."

"No, not nearly as often as I wanted. But my mom had good reason to want us to be nicer than most. She told me that since I was a cat, I'd have to be nice to people. Otherwise they'd be thinking that we're all monsters—that we only want to hurt. Then about two months before I was to retire from the force, a shifter—a cat too, but a tiger—went nuts and killed several people in a hotel that dealt by the hour, and not usually by the night." She asked him why. "Well, I'm not telling you this story to make you come to me, but his mate, a woman of some repute, had told him that she wanted other lovers. It was her job, you see. Anyway, I guess, because he loved her, that he thought that he could let her do what she seemed to enjoy. I don't know how he thought that would work, but then she was killed by one of the men."

"Oh, how terrible. Would you let me do that?" He simply said no. "Finish the story before I have to tell you how I don't like that word."

"All right. Okay, so she had all these lovers, and one of them supposedly killed her. He was distraught. His heart was broken, and he decided that he wanted to die, by the police. It happens a great deal. When he decided to rob a bank, that's where I stepped in." She had forgotten he was a cop. "You see, I had just seen his mate not two days before working a street in another town that my brothers and I had gone shopping in. When I asked him if he was planning to join her, he said yes, thinking to die. But when I told him that she wasn't gone, he went a little berserk, hurting everyone around him and killing several more when he found her in another hotel with several men. At once."

30

"You were hurt." He nodded at her. "And you what? Killed him too. Surely they saw that as self-defense, didn't they?"

"Oh yes. I was cleared of the charges of killing him, almost immediately. But in my need to heal myself, I shifted. It was that or die. And people saw me." She nodded, terrified of what he'd just said. "I was, politely mind you, asked to step down and retire. So, since I was ready to do it anyway, I did, and moved back home. It was the best...well, the second-best thing that has happened to me."

"Me being one of them." He told her she was the first, along with Ruby. "I'm not ready for that, I don't think. I'm a woman who for the most part stayed by myself. The only reason that I was with Kenneth was that it was going to be beneficial for us both. We wanted our careers more than we wanted a home life. Then there was the added fact that his lover, who was also a good friend, wanted a child. Ruby isn't either of theirs, but an artificially implanted baby that they were to raise. I had no trouble with that—I had my focus on other things. The money would have paid down my debt from med school, and I would have been there to help them raise her. But he was killed."

"Do you think that Dexter did it?"

Ruby had long since fallen asleep, but when she moved her to lay her down, Jules took her and turned his back so that she could adjust her clothing. It was too much, to have a man like this want to be there for her all the time. Tess felt tears gather in her eyes as she answered his question.

"We weren't married. Everyone thinks that we were. Even, I think, Dexter. But the baby wasn't supposed to....

31

What I mean to say is, these things usually take time, to have a child this way. I got it in one. And after that, things started to surge forward faster. I wanted Dexter to give me away; he is…was my best friend. But when I told him about the baby he went a little nuts. I was knocked out. And when I woke, Kenneth was dead, and I was alone." He asked her about the lover. "Daniel. Daniel killed himself a few weeks after the funeral. He couldn't take it, losing his lover, the responsibility of a child. He left her everything, but because of the fact that we weren't married either, his family fought for it and won. Ruby is all that I have."

"What does he do? Dexter. What does he do when he sees you?" Tess asked if they could do this later, she was starving. "Of course. I forgot about that. Come on, we'll have some dinner, then we'll see what you want of the things in the house. You don't have to stay there. I'd like it, but you don't have to. The room, as far as I can remember — I've only been in it once — looks like it's never been used. For all I know, none of it has been."

His family had not only waited on them to join them, but had also been very busy. Mrs. Stanton had a day bed set up for Ruby to sleep in when she visited, and a plethora of other items that she'd love as well. It looked like, to Tess, that they had adopted them both, and her granddad could not be happier for them. Tess was still trying to figure this all out.

Willing to go to his home, just to see what she could use at the hotel, Tess knew that Jules had to know it all. Not just that she really did think that Dexter had killed Kenneth, but all the other stuff that was going on as well. Like the money that kept coming up missing.

Chapter 3

The surgery was set for this morning, but Kendal wasn't sure that this was a good idea. He was feeling better, and his head didn't hurt nearly so much now. But his wife, Sandra, told him if he backed out of this, she'd have his head hurting more than it was now. She was not one to mess with.

"Mr. Wayne?" He looked at the beautiful woman standing in his room and smiled his greeting while taking Sandra's hand. "My name is Dr. Tess O'Rourke. My granddad is going to be doing your surgery, but he's running a little late today. I'm sorry. As soon as he gets here, we'll begin. Did you have any questions for me?"

"You think this will work, Dr. O'Rourke? I mean, those other doctors have told me that it would kill me to have it removed. That I might be a vegetable or something." He looked at his wife. "We've not been able to start a family because we were so worried about her having to do everything on her own and care for me too."

"Kendal, my granddad is the best there is at working on the brain. You should have no fear on that. And if he thinks that it'll harm you more than you have been, I promise you that he'll stop and not do any damage to you." He nodded. "Let me give you some information that you might not have gotten from the other doctors. Once the bullet is removed, you'll need to recuperate for a while. Not as long as you might have by being a wolf, but you will need to not shift for at least a few weeks. At least until the bone is set."

"They said that they'd have to cut into my noodle." Tess laughed and told him that was right. That was why he'd been shaved. "Yeah, that's not so comfy. I'm wondering if my wolf will be bald as well."

"I have no idea. That's a good question, but don't go trying to figure that out. We need you healthy and strong. This surgery is going to take a few hours. Then you'll be in recovery for a few hours after that. I'll keep Sandra updated while my granddad works, but you can rest assured, both of us have done this several times and we're very good. That's why Dr. Stanton called him in."

When she left him, he looked at his lovely wife. "We'll have a baby when you go into heat next. And I'll be home to help you all the time." She laid her head on his chest and he held her. "Mr. Stanton came in last night. He said that he'd meant to come in earlier, but he'd gotten sidetracked. He offered me a job when this is finished."

"They gave me one too. And while at first, I thought it was a pity job, but it's not. I feel needed, Ken. Like I've never felt at other jobs. They put me in charge of procurement of supplies for the new center." He hugged her, afraid of what might happen if he didn't pull through this thing. "Don't think like that. You're going to be just fine. Like she told us, they've done this before. We'll be just fine."

"I'm still worried about you." She said she wasn't going to leave at all. "You'd better not sit here for eight hours, honey. Go have some lunch with that friend of yours."

"She isn't very helpful, nor is she all that nice either. And her husband is all huffy because I have a good job now." Ken asked her what she meant. "Shirley is telling me that I'm a fool for allowing you to do this. That you are going to be a burden more so than you are now to me. And after I told her, in no uncertain words, you were not a burden, she put that little nose of hers in the air and left in a huff. I decided I need better friends. Like the Stantons."

He started to caution her about making friends out of their reach, then remembered what Levi had told him when he'd come to offer him the job yesterday. It started off with him calling him by his first name, then went downhill, as far as Ken was concerned, from there.

"What do you mean, I'm your better? Better at what?" Kendall told him. "This is the twentieth century; you are aware of that, aren't you? I'm a person, just like you, with issues, bills, and everything that goes with that. I'm just a man, like you, a shifter man that has a little more money. And with that, I'm going to help you because I like you. If you ever say that to my parents, however, I will put flowers on your grave and tell you that you fucked up."

They were both laughing by the time he convinced him that they were equals. The job was for him to come to his office every day and help him with cleanup. And while it did sound

35

like a crappy job, Levi told Kendall he didn't know what sort of a slob he was. Levi showed him pictures of his work area, and Ken wasn't sure that he could even do that for him.

"I need you. I have a couple of shows coming up soon. One of them is in Germany and then the other is local, as in the States. You'd have to go with me to those too. I mean, you could stay home. But if you do, then we'll have to work out something. I'd be grateful. My parents would be grateful as well." He asked about his house. "My house is immaculate. I have a butler and a housekeeper. If not, then I'd hate to think what sort of mess I'd have there. Probably some kind of science project too."

When Levi left an hour later, leaving behind a check and some cash, Ken stared at it for several minutes before he called his banker and told him what had happened. The man didn't seem to know anything about it until he was put on hold for a moment.

"Mr. Stanton just came in and set you up on his payroll, Mr. Wayne. He suggested that if you needed me to come over and pick up the money and check, I could do that for you." Mr. Wayne? He'd been everything but a mister since he'd gotten back from the Army. "You just let me know if I can do anything else for you. Oh, and your house loan is paid off, as well as the back taxes. You are free and clear with us."

Free and clear. He'd not been clear with anyone since he'd been eighteen and joined the service. Now he was caught up on his house, his car was no longer in threat of being repossessed, and he had money in his account. He wondered what sort of person did that to a near stranger. Holding his wife, he told her what had been done.

"Really?" He nodded. "My goodness. This is.... How do we pay them back?" He told her what Levi had told him. That to mention it would be a breach of good manners. "Good manners. I don't think when my momma was beating those into me, she ever mentioned paying someone's loan off and not bringing it up again."

"Maybe because, like with us, there was never a chance for it to happen." Sandra said that was right, and laid her head back down on his chest. "I'm worried about this. You're to move on if I die. I don't want you to go out and end your own life."

"I won't." He laughed. "What a thing to say to me right before they pop your skull open like a can opener. You're going to be fine. I'm going to be fine. All of us are." He said he hoped so. "Me too, but we have to believe it, Ken. If not, then why bother?"

A few minutes before noon, a man came to get him. They were going to prep him for surgery. And Sandra wasn't able to go with him. Almost as soon as he was in the next phase of the hospital, Dr. O'Rourke came to see him. The mister this time.

"I've fallen and broken my wrist." Ken said he was sorry to hear that, then asked when they were going to reschedule. "No need for it if you're willing to have my granddaughter operate. She's good, if not better than me. And she's younger. These old bones aren't as strong as they used to be."

"She's all right with this?" Dr. O'Rourke said that Tess was more than all right with it. "All right then, but don't tell my wife. She's nervous enough as it is. I don't want her thinking that this is an omen or something."

"I won't. I'll assist, in that I'll be there with Tess, but she'll do the operation. You have nothing to worry about, Ken. She's better than I am, like I said." He nodded as the nurse told him he was going to feel slightly lightheaded. "Go on now, let the drugs take you while they prep you the rest of the way."

He did feel woozy, but not too badly. When they asked him if he could move, he tried, but he wasn't sure if he could have made his arms move. Suddenly in the air for a moment, he felt the softness of the bed under him, then Tess was there.

"Hello, Ken. How are you feeling?" He must have answered her because she told him she was glad. "I'm going to put you under for a little while, then about halfway through, I'm going to wake you up, talk to you a little bit, then you'll go to sleep, all right?"

"Yes, whatever you need. You're very pretty, did you know that?" She laughed, and he felt silly. "I'm sorry. I'm not feeling myself."

"Well, we'll get you there. You just hold on for me." He felt the magic of meds go over him. When he closed his eyes, the entire world seemed to just go away. Even the pain in his head was gone. His last thoughts were, he sure hoped he felt this good when this was finished.

~~~

Tess washed her hands three times. The happiness was making her old habits start up again, and instead of feeling terrible, she felt like a million bucks. Her granddad joined her a few minutes after she was drying up.

"You did wonderful in there." Thanking him, she realized that it was the first time that they'd worked together. "I had no idea that you'd gotten that perfect at this. Even his wound

38

is going to heal much better once he can shift."

"I was concerned that he'd have speech trouble when he couldn't talk there for a minute." Granddad nodded. "Then we just lowered the meds more and there he was. I think he's going to be just fine now, don't you?"

"I do. But this has gotten me to thinking. I think it's about time that I hang up my scalpel." He'd said that before, but now it sounded different, like he meant it. Before she could tell him no, he spoke again. "I'm not going to stop taking in patients, honey, just not operate any more. I want you and me to go into practice together. We work as a team, you get your name out there, and before you know it, I can stay home with Ruby and any other children that you and Jules have, and be the best great grandda there ever was."

"I'm not ready for this. I mean, you know what I have going on." He said he was no longer worried about that. "I am. You know what sort of person Dexter can be. And now that he's free to roam around like he owns me, he's never going to stop."

"You think that Jules or any of the rest of them is going to allow you to be hurt? They won't. And Ruby could not be in better hands unless she was with you. Lucy is even teaching her to call her Grandma. Have you been to see the house that Jules owns?"

"No, not yet. Last night Ruby was so exhausted that I couldn't leave her. And this morning Jules had some work to do at the office. Did you know that he was a beat cop turned PI?" He said that he did. "Dane said that she's looking into Dexter for me, but I don't know what she'll find from there. He was never like this before his mom died."

"I think there's more to that than we know as well." Tess asked him what. "I don't know, but something. I'll let you go for now, honey. You go and talk to Sandra and let her know that he's come through with flying colors. All right?"

After she changed her shirt, she made her way to the lobby. Tess was surprised to see Jules there, with Ruby sleeping on his chest and him sleeping with her. The two of them looked as if they really could be father and daughter. When Sandra said her name, she moved with her to the next room and smiled.

"Ken, he's all right?" Tess told her what they'd done and how he'd done too. "I'm so happy. I guess he's going to be out for a while, correct?"

"Yes, a few more hours. I want him rested so that he doesn't try and harm himself." She wanted to let the woman go so she could go and watch Jules and Ruby. She must have looked funny, because Sandra laughed. "I'm sorry. Did I miss something?"

"He's been playing with her since he brought her in. And he got her to stand up next to the table. She was wobbly, but he had so many nurses coming to see her that you'd think she walked. Anyway, the two of them have been sleeping for the last half hour. I took pictures. I'll send them to you." Tess thanked her and gave her a card with her personal email on it. "Jules is a good man. And you couldn't ask for a better family to be a part of. I've known of the Stantons my entire life. And if you ever needed something, they'd be there for you. No matter what."

"He's taking me to see his home today." She said it was massive. "That's what he said. And that for the most part, there is a lot of furniture still in it. A pink bedroom for Ruby too."

"I knew the Jacobs. A nice woman she wasn't. The mister was nice enough, but they thought that they were so much better than anyone that came around. My mom used to cook and clean for them. Nothing was ever good enough for her. And the mister had some kind of phobia where he was fearful that there were germs in his bathroom. Mom had to use all kinds of cleaners in there just to make him happy." Tess asked her about the baby. "It wasn't his. The wife had had numerous affairs even before they were married, and when he figured out the truth about the baby, he kicked her to the curb, so to speak. But the judge decided that there was too much anger for them to divide things up equally, so he ordered the house and contents to be sold. Jules asked what the buying price was and bought it. He offered Mr. Jacobs anything he wanted, but he said there was nothing in the house that he needed now that he was moving on. Good for the both of you, I think."

"I'll let you know." She looked at the other woman. "I don't have any friends in this town. I was wondering if you'd be one for me. You can say no if you want. Though I don't know why you'd want to—"

"We are friends, Tess. And I'm honored, even if you didn't know, that we are. Thank you." Tess told her she was sorry. "No reason to be. I think it's great. And with you and Jules being a couple, maybe, if I can get my husband out of the house again, we can do things together."

"I'd like that too."

She made her way to her daughter then she lifted her head up off of Jules's chest. She thought that she could just take her and let him sleep, but he grabbed her arm before she got her loose. Fear was on his face before his grip loosened and he smiled at her.

"I didn't want to wake you."

"That's okay. I wasn't fully asleep anyway. She snores." For some reason that made her laugh. "How did things go? Is Ken going to have a better life?"

"Oh, I hope so, but we'll have to wait. I didn't know what to do with the bullet, so I did the whole chain of command thing and had my granddad put it in his safe. I'm not sure what it might be needed for, but when we have that sort of thing happen, we make sure that it's done well for court, if it comes to that." He told her he'd send someone for it. "I'm starving."

"Good. How about I take my two favorite girls out to dinner?" He took Ruby from her and smelled her butt like a pro. "I guess we need to freshen up. You do your thing, we'll do ours. And so you know, Ruby is a real flirt. She had anyone that walked by eating right out of her hands."

She went to take a shower and to change after talking to the staff and giving them Jules's number. Tess would need a cell phone soon if this became something she did for Granddad.

As she was dressing in her street clothing, she heard her name being yelled from the locker room.

"Tess? Where the fuck are you? They said you were up here. Yoohoo? Tess? Come out, come out, where ever you are." She was terrified, and in that moment, she knew that the next time she was with Jules, she was going to have him bite her. Then she could be found. "Tessie, where are you, goddamn it? This is fucking bullshit. Where the fuck are you? And you'd better have that brat with you. I have told Dexter several times, no kids."

Told Dexter? She didn't understand, and thought perhaps she'd heard him wrong. As she backed deeper into the room, she could hear him yelling for her in the same singsong voice of his.

Tess had gotten dressed in the shower room, so her locker was open and all her things were on the bench. Tess heard them crash to the floor just as Dexter came around the corner. He lunged at her, knocking her back against the wall, and everything went black. But she heard him, just as clear as day, saying over and over, "No kids, no kids, no kids."

~~~

Dexter tried his best to wake Tessie up, but she was bleeding really bad. He was panicking now, his heart racing. What if he had killed her? he asked his mom. She didn't want her dead, just the kid. The little girl was unsafe with his mom around, and he knew it. What to do, he hadn't any idea.

"No kids. No kids." He heard it over and over while he found a towel and laid it over Tess's face. Then that freaked him out a little, so he just wrapped it round her head. *"Too much this time, Dexter. I told you to behave with women, didn't I? You have never been a very good boy, and even with you being the son of God, you still manage to fuck things up."*

"You did this, not me, Mom. Why do you constantly want to hurt her? She's done nothing to you." His mom told him that she had a kid, and she had told him once, or a thousand times, no kids, no kids, no kids. "It's not my child, you know that. Why don't you just leave them both alone? Now look what you've done. You've hurt her, and now she'll die."

"I see it all, Dexter Shipley and you'd better remember that. And why shouldn't she die? I think that anyone that has a child, they should die with it. They're nasty, and the Lord has told me so. You have to get me that child, Dexter." He told her he was sorry, but he wasn't going to do that. "You'd better do what I tell you to do or else. Get out of here before you're caught. Go now before someone comes."

Dexter left then, running down the hall. Seeing the doctors coming his way, he moved into one of the big rooms that his mom told him was empty. How she knew these things, when she wouldn't even tell him where she was in person, he didn't know, but Dexter's mother was all he had. She must have told him that fifty times a day.

"Get to the house and pack you a bag." He said that he would, and then asked her where he was going. "I don't know. You just go home; it'll take you some time, so when you get there, I want you to be careful that no one is in there waiting for you. You know what will happen if you're caught, don't you? I'll never get to talk to you again. They'll take out your brain. Not that you have much use for it anyway."

Dexter told his mom he was sorry about that, but ran like his life depended on it. He was sure that he'd killed Tessie, and all he'd wanted to do was to talk to her. But she was always with that baby. If she was with the baby when he found her, his mother would make him take her. And he didn't want to hurt either of them. But the baby — the word hurt his head. Terrible pain took his breath away.

"No. No kids, Dexter. How many times do I have to tell you that? Run through that grocery store. That'll slow them down." He did as he was told, knocking over a stand of chips while he was running. *"You ignorant fool. What is wrong with you? Walk now, and be quick about it."*

Walking gave him time to think. His head was hurting really badly again, and when he stopped near the new building they were putting up, he closed his eyes and asked Mom to give him a moment or two. She was making him hurt in the belly too.

For some reason she did as he'd asked this time, being quiet so that he could rest. Thinking about poor Tessie, he wondered if she was going to be all right. He needed her. She was a doctor, and he needed her to help him.

Dexter had been such a smart person when he'd been living at home. His mom had told everyone that he was. He'd graduated from high school at fifteen. He'd gotten into college not long after, and had excelled there as well. Graduating from Harvard, he'd been ready to start his life.

But Dexter knew that he'd never find a girl and bring her home. Not then. His dreams had been shattered, if he'd ever had any, of having a family as well as a home with children. Those things had never been a part of his life since she'd hurt him one day when he'd been a teenager. After that, Dexter couldn't get far enough away from her.

It took him a long time to want to come home. He wasn't sure why he had—something to do with a person. But his mind didn't go there. He knew that something had happened and it was bad, but he couldn't, or perhaps didn't want to, think about it. But after a few years of just living in his house, someone wanted to meet her. His nose started bleeding when he tried to make himself remember. And when bits and pieces of it came to him, he would feel his belly lurch up and he'd be sick again. He wished that he could remember something about this other person.

"No, no, no, no." Dexter tried to make his head stop spinning; the colors hurt because they were so bright. And when he blacked out, his head just too much for him, the dream or thoughts, he wasn't sure which, started again. But he knew someone was going to find him and put him away. Just like his mom told him they would for what he'd done.

"*Look at this mess, Dexter. This is all your fault.*" He couldn't see what he'd done, but then, he didn't remember doing anything to anyone. "*If anyone finds out what you did, what do you think they're going to do to you? I'll tell you, they'll lock you away for good. Not even being the son of God will help you with this.*"

"No, I don't see it." He could see the bed, the floor, but nothing on it. Like it was all rubbed out. "Mom, where is Alma?"

"*She's a bad girl. You're better off without her. She's gone.*" He asked again where she'd gone. "*Never you mind, you just clean this mess up.*"

He didn't see a mess. He didn't seem to be able to remember things. Just knew that she was his Alma. It bothered him to no end that he couldn't remember where she'd gone with their child. As for the mess, Dexter might have seen it then, but now all he could remember was picking up the blankets and sheets and putting them in the trash bags. Then since the weather was just perfect, Mom told him to burn the trash. He did that in the night, because the lights were so pretty when they sparkled in the sky. That, he remembered.

Moving slower now, he made his way to the bus station. Mom told him that he'd have to hit the bank again when he got there. She used to work there, at the same one that Tessie had her account in, so she told him how to get the money out. Tessie didn't need money, Mom told him. She didn't know how to manage it correctly. He didn't believe that, but he had to do what she told him or he'd have problems. Painful ones. So every week, he'd go and get her cash out and the tellers would never say a word.

The bus trip took him the better part of the night. He saw the police lights there when they pulled in, and he did what his mom told him. Slipping out the back window of the bus, he was gone before they boarded, and was on his way to his home. There he would eat, rest, and be on his way to the bank first thing in the morning. Taking out the credit card, he looked at the name on it, and wondered, not for the first time over the months, who this Alma person was and why he had her credit card.

"You never mind about her. I told you, she was a bad girl. You need to work on getting that child from Tess. That child will be your ticket to Heaven. The Lord told me so. Without a kid, you're just like everyone else. Lazy. And my Lord does not like lazy people. Give me that child, Dexter. I've told you before. You never listen to me. Did you hear me, Dexter? You will not make me a grandma before I'm ready. I mean it. No kids, no kids, no kids." He told her he knew that, but getting the baby was hard. *"You just work harder at getting her, and then bring her right to me. I know just what to do with the little thing."*

Dexter's mind skittered across something horrific. He only saw it for the briefest of moments, then it was gone. Going into the living room, he sat there in the darkness waiting for the sun to come up. First thing, he was going to the bank. Then he had to make the trip back to Tessie and her baby. He had to warn them all.

"Why can't I just keep the baby?" She told him that she didn't like children. "I know, but you're not here right now. I can just not bring her over to see you and care for her myself. She's a pretty little thing, and I think—"

"*And how will Tess feel about that? You already killed off her husband, that bad man, didn't you?*" He wasn't so sure about that either. Someone had killed him, but Dexter wasn't the murdering type; someone had told him that. "*You probably killed Tess. I think that makes you a murderer, don't you?*"

Rocking back and forth as he used to do as a child when things got too stressful, he started saying the presidents of the United States and the years they were in office. When that list was finished, he started on other lists, other things to keep his mom out of his head.

Dexter could think really well this way while his mind was working out another problem. But his mom, she couldn't get into his head while he was doing it. He figured she might one day, but for now, his thoughts were his own. And he had to think what happened to the other person and Kenneth. He'd liked him, and now he was gone too. Too many things going on that he couldn't remember. Too many things. But first and foremost, he had to warn Tessie, to tell her to run with her little girl. Not to ever allow his mom to watch or even to touch her. Something was wrong, and he didn't know what. Only that she'd hurt her if she could.

Chapter 4

Jules didn't want to leave her, but knew that he had to do something productive. But almost as soon as he stood up, thinking that he'd take a walk around the nurses' station again, Tess opened her eyes.

"Hello, beautiful. I'm so glad to see you." She grinned, then winced. "Yeah, you should probably just lie still for a little while longer. You have a nice bruise on your cheek there; not too bad, but it will be sore. Plus, they had to put nineteen stitches in the back of your head, and even then, it was still a worrisome knot."

"Ruby?" He had to hold her down while he told her that her daughter was with his mom. "I was so afraid that he'd find the two of you. Dexter, he was.... I want you to find him, Jules. There is something wrong with him. I don't know what, but he's not the same person he was before. He's more...I don't know, like he's not all there. Childlike. That's it; he's more childlike than I remember him being."

"Dane, you've met her, she's been doing some research, and you know some of it. That his mom is dead, but what you don't know is what a sick evil bitch she might have been. If you promise to rest here, I'm going to tell you what we've been able to piece together. And before you try to convince me that he needs help, I believe you. There are things...things going on that you're not going to believe, all right?" She told him yes. "All right. We know where he is right now—at his home that he shared with Alma. And it was more than just a casual relationship between them. He purchased an engagement ring for her, and more than likely gave it to her. They were content. More than content—we think he and Alma were very happy to be a couple. That is, until he took her home to meet his mom."

"Debra Jorden wasn't a nice person. I don't think anyone knew that as well as me and Dexter did." He told her no shit. "But she's dead. How or what does any of this have to do with her?"

"When Dexter started dating Alma, he was very careful that his mother didn't know. Also, the people that he worked with were surprised that he even had a living mom. It wasn't until he took Alma to his mom's home that they realized that she was still around. And only then because he had to ask for time off." He didn't want to tell her this but knew that she had been friends with Dexter until recently. "Alma was excited, as you can guess. Her friends, people that she worked with, were in turn very excited for her. To meet the parents was a big deal. Before leaving, Dexter proposed and set things up so that they'd marry when they returned. As you can guess, it never happened. Alma was five months pregnant."

"No." He nodded. "I don't want to know the rest. Not now. She did something to that baby, didn't she? And to Alma. What was it? Please, tell me."

"She lost the child, as best we can tell. How, we're not sure, but she said that it wasn't an accident. So—this is just speculation on Dane's part—Debra didn't want her son to be married, nor to have a child. She didn't want to be a grandmother at all. Her neighbors said that Debra told them that all the time, that she'd rather be dead then be called Grandma. So, she took care that she wasn't one. We believe, and Dane is rarely wrong about this sort of thing, but she thinks that she strapped Alma to a bed then cut the child out of her, and she died along with her child. She murdered them both." Jules watched her face; he knew this was too much, but he had to tell her all of it. "Dane went to the house where things had happened and had a team go over everything. There is blood in one of the bedrooms consistent with what she thinks happened."

"Oh, poor Dexter. Do you think that he knew? That he was there when that happened?" Jules told her that for the most part Dexter didn't spend much time at his mother's home when visiting. "He would have snapped after that—is that what you're saying happened?"

"Dexter and Alma spent a lot of time away from the house. It was only for four days, but on the last day, Dexter was alone. Up until then she was going to have the baby, and people were surprised when she wasn't with him the last day. He told people that she was resting up and packing. He was picking up a few things for his mother. Dexter doesn't go there. His mind snapped after that, as you have surmised.

He hasn't been the same man he'd been before, as you know. And when asked about Alma, he doesn't know. While Dane is reasonably sure that he didn't have anything to do with her death or that of his child, he did help with the cleanup. They burned the rags and such in the back yard. The body was buried nearby with the child."

"Oh no—no, that's so not right, Jules. You have to have it wrong. Tell Dane to keep looking. There has to be a better reason that that poor woman and her child are gone. Please, tell her." He held her why she cried. "My poor friend. She did this to him, didn't she? Debra was a horrid person when we were children, but I never expected her to be a murderer. Oh no, I just remembered something. When I was falling backward, I heard him say 'no kids,' but it was different."

"How do you mean different?" They both looked at his dad and Colton when they entered the room. Colton asked Tess again what she meant by him being different. "He talks to himself, or so we thought, but now we're not so sure. I think he might be talking to his dead mother, as well as answering himself with her voice."

"He's being his mom?" Colton nodded. "No. He never liked his mom. I mean, I knew her too, when we were younger. But she's dead."

"If what I've heard is true, when she made him help her with the clean up or more, his mind took a turn so that he wouldn't have to remember what had happened. To Alma, or about the cleanup afterwards. He was, for all intents and purposes, an extremely bright man. Graduated from college. Had a good job. They even owned the house that they lived in. And when he met up with his mom, he never mentioned any of these things." She asked him how he knew. "We found Debra's diary. Or I should say diaries. Not once does she mention a woman, nor does she say a word about him having a home. Because we think she didn't have any idea, not until he brought Alma home to meet her. That's important, because she does talk about everything else, and had kept a running diary since he was born. Every year since he'd been born, she kept a catalog of events of his entire life. And according to her notes, Debra didn't even know that she was to have a child until she gave birth to it one night in her bed. No one assisted her, and there wasn't any kind of birth certificate. It wasn't until he was ready to go to school that she applied for one, having to remember as many details as she could. But there is no mention of a father. Not even an unknown."

"So, she killed this woman because of a baby, then she had Dexter help with the disposal of the body and the child, and then what? He killed her? Debra died not long after I found out I was pregnant with Ruby." She looked like she was thinking hard. "From what I remember, it was thought it was a heart attack and that she died at home alone. But I don't know. I do remember thinking that perhaps Dexter could get his life together now that his mom was gone. But to be honest with you, I didn't know Alma. After he went to college, we sort of went our separate ways. Do you think it was the baby that sent him after me?"

"I don't know. I think you'd be better equipped to answer that. But I will say this—whatever is wrong with Dexter right now, it's because of his mom. The things that we've read in those diaries of hers are sick." Julian asked his brother how many diaries there were. "One for each year of his life. And there are pictures too. She did things to him—had him shave his pubic hair off when he was ten. Pluck out his underarm hair when he was about the same age. She even made him wear girls' panties when he woke up with a hard on. The woman was a sadist. And through it all, she maintained a façade of being the perfect mother of a very smart young man. He never once hinted of the life he had there, other than to you."

"She killed that poor baby and its mom. Oh my God, Jules, I just thought of something. She murdered her own grandchild." Colton looked at him when Tess spoke. "What is it? What else have you found out?"

"Dexter is still writing in diaries. He has taken over for his mother. He is his mother when he writes in them. They're all over the house where he's at. Bits and pieces of what he's done all day, and how he's got to keep babies away from her little boy. That's how we found out the other things too, like why he is taking your cash. Why he wants the baby dead. Not you—he won't kill you, even though his mom says for him to. He won't do it. He loves you like a sister. But we honestly believe, from when his mind takes over from his mom, that he's trying to protect Ruby from her."

Jules wanted to tell Colton to stop, that this was too much, but all he did was look at him and tell him what he thought. "You can't hurt this man. He's not guilty of any of this. Not hurting the baby, not what he did to Tess. This is a problem that started well before his mom was killed." Jules looked at Tess. "Colton and my dad, they're the best at what they do. So, if they have a plan, we should do it. I don't want him hurt any more than you do, love."

"Who killed Debra, do you know?" Colton nodded at Tess. "He killed her, didn't he? That's what you're trying very hard not to tell me. Somehow he made it look like she had a heart attack, and he killed her."

"Yes. He killed her about the same time that Alma died. The child, a little boy, he died soon after being born, but not long after. He was too small." Jules reached for and caught Tess's hand in his own as his dad continued. "The family is going to be notified today about their daughter. There won't be any information about her just yet, not in the papers either. The police will just tell them that it's an ongoing investigation, and they'll tell them that while we don't have any suspects at this time, we're very close. We have to see if we can bring Dexter in without hurting him."

"But you know where he is. You said he was at his home." Dad nodded at Tess. "Then I don't understand. Why not just go and get him and bring him in and talk to him? Maybe we can get him some help."

But Jules knew the answer and looked at Tess. "He'll never understand what's going on. He hasn't any idea that Alma is dead, that his child is either. The mind is a tricky thing. The trauma of all this, it's put him in a place where he's safe from thinking about what has happened to them." Colton said that he hadn't mentioned the child when writing as his mom. "So, there isn't anything we can get him help for without him being Dexter. What I mean is —"

"He could become his mother and never come out of this at all." He nodded. "The mind is a complicated and delicate thing. If he reverts to his mother, he'll never be able to remember what he was like before this. Have no idea about

Alma loving him. Or the baby that they more than likely loved. Being his mom might be safe for him, but it'll never help him grieve."

"That's right. The house, it was ready for the baby. They knew it was a boy as well. But it's closed off; there is even a chair in front of the door, almost to remind him, or his mind, not to go there." Tess started crying, but Colton didn't stop. "The things in the house, they were beautiful. Poems. There was a date on the calendar for appointments, and he was going with her to all of them. Then they just stopped. The calendar is still on the time they went to see his mom, months ago. It's also marked with the time they were going to be getting married. When they returned."

After his brother left them, taking Dad home too, he held onto Tess for over an hour. She would speak about how Dexter had been her friend, things they'd done as children. But then she'd sob again about how his mother was such a horrible person. Through it all, she kept holding his hand.

"I want you to make me like you." He nodded, not really sure she was paying attention to what she was saying. "When I was there in the bathroom that day, all I could think about was how you wouldn't have been able to find me. That if I was killed, you'd never know it. And I vowed that I wanted you to bite me, but now I want you to convert me. I need to have something extra to keep me from being a victim."

"We'll need to wait until you're released before I can convert you. But as for taking a bite of you, I can do that. I'd willingly bite you now." She smiled a watery smile at him. "Tess, I love you so much. I'd very much like for you to be my wife before this all hits the fan."

"I'm good with that." He laughed, and she did as well. "I know that's not really a very good way to say yes, but you understand."

"I do. I can have us a license in about twenty-four hours. Mom and your granddad can get all the planning done. I'm guessing you want him to give you away?" She said that she did, and to have Ruby in the wedding as well. "Good. And if you would let me, I'd like to adopt her. To give you both my last name."

"Yes, all right." He cocked a brow at her. "I'm sorry. *Woohoo! Yes, I'll marry you and let you give your name to my little girl!* How was that?"

"Much better." He got up and went to his jacket, and when he returned he had a small box that had a pretty, gold ribbon on the top. "I saw this and thought of you. And I'm having a bracelet made for Ruby too."

The diamond ring was gorgeous. There were small rubies all around the diamond that sat in a Tiffany setting on a wide band. She noticed, too, that it seemed to be broken, and asked him about it.

"No, not broken, but it is open at the back so that when you shift, if you ever do, then you'll not lose a finger while doing it. You see, this will stretch and once you're fitted with it, a small bit of gold, very little, is inserted in the slice so that no one but us will know its purpose." He slipped it on her finger. "Just as I thought. A tiny finger. I love you, Tess O'Rourke. Would you please consent to be my wife?"

"Yes. When? I know you said a few hours, but I have a feeling that you have a license already filled out and ready for me to sign." Jules got up to get the license, and about that time, Brayden and Dane walked in with a minster. They were ready to be married as soon as her granddad showed up with little Ruby. "This is perfect. I didn't want large anyway."

"My mom has a different opinion. So if you really don't want a large wedding later, then you're the one who's going to tell her. I'm not." The minister started speaking, and a young man interrupted them with more paperwork. It was handed to Dane.

"Just in time. All you need to do, Tess, is sign where the tabs are, and little Ruby Denise O'Rourke will be called Ruby Denise Stanton." She signed where she'd been told, and then Jules did the same. He stared at the paperwork for several minutes before giving it back to Dane. "It'll be filed within the next hour and you'll be a family. Congratulations."

"We have to sort of marry first."

They all laughed, and in ten minutes, Jules had a wife and daughter. He was as happy as he'd ever been in his life.

~~~

Christian looked over the paperwork twice before setting it aside. He wasn't sure this was really what his brother wanted. Not like this. Looking at Julian, he wasn't even sure now that his brother even wanted to work at all. Not as a cop again, anyway.

"What is it you want?" Julian asked him what he meant. "Besides working for the city, which I don't believe you want to do. What do you want? It's not the pay. This is less than you were making on unemployment when you could have gotten it. It can't be the hours either. They're long, and you only have one day on the weekend off. So tell me, little brother, what do you want from this job?"

"To get out of the house while Tess isn't there." Therein lay the issue. "I'm bored, if you want to know the truth of it. I started watching television, those daytime things that drive you nuts when you miss one. I need something to do."

"What about the PI stuff? I thought you enjoyed that." He told him he thought it was depressing. "And Ruby, what do you want done with her while you work?"

His entire face lit up when Christian mentioned her name. He loved the little girl as much as he did the mom. Which was understandable. The child had taken to Julian as if she had known what a special person he was going to be in her life.

"I want to stay with her all day, but I can't do that either. I know that. It's mind starving to be with her. Understand?" He did. "So I need something to get me out of the house and with people of the same age. Maybe not the same age, but at least someone I can talk to. And this will do it."

"This will get you killed. And if not killed, you'd be in danger every single day you strap on that gun." Jules lifted his shirt up and Christian saw the gun there, then he put his boot up and there was another one there. "If you show me one more, I'm going to call Mom and tell her you're getting ready for the zombie invasion."

"What can I do, Christian? I'm seriously bored out of my mind. I've been a working person almost my entire life. And now, all I do is get in the way of the cook. And if not that, the rest of the staff." He wiped his face with his hand. "What do you think I should do?"

"Okay, this is a long shot, but I know you have a master's in law. You also have a master's in history. Have you thought of being a teacher?" His face told him that there wasn't any way in hell he wanted to teach. "All right. Tell me what kind of things you enjoy doing. We'll start from there. And just so you know, if you don't come up with something by my next appointment, I'm kicking your ass out. I do like what I do, and I'm very good at it."

Just as he was opening his mouth, a sharp knock came to the door, and in walked the mayor. Just what he needed right now. The loud-mouthed sap of an idiot coming in to bother him again. The guy had been here every day since rumor had it that he, Christian Stanton, had been asked to be the mayor.

As soon as he sat down, Julian pointed at him and nodded.

"I didn't know you were having a meeting. Are the two of you plotting to take my place? I'm telling you right now, and I've said this before, Christian, you just don't understand the differences between being mayor and being an attorney." He told him he wasn't running against him. "I'm glad to hear that, I am. I love my job. And I'm sure you love yours. But I keep hearing rumors about you plotting."

"Plotting? You've said that twice now." Christian leaned back in his seat to watch his brother. Julian was good at this, getting to the root of all problems. "What is it you think he'd have to do to plot anything? Print up a few signs? Go to the ladies' meetings and scarf up a nice lunch? I've seen you at them, Mayor Windbag—you're not all that articulate. I think they only invite you when they know they don't want to have any leftovers. Is it true that you bring your own containers and take whatever is left home with you?"

"A man has to eat. And I've told you this before, Jules, my name is Windbreeze, not Windbag. Why do you have so much trouble with that?" He looked at Christian then. "I just don't want to come up to election day and see that you've put out your signs."

"I would think he'd need a few more days than that, don't you? I mean, just think about it. Printing alone would be a nightmare. While Christian takes a good photo, he would need an ad campaign and someone to help him with that. Oh wait, he has one. We have a brother that's an artist." Jules laughed. "You know, I should run against you. I was just telling my brother that I have nothing to do all day. I mean, according to your schedule of events, I'm sure I'd have time to play with my new daughter and be around my brain surgeon of a wife."

"You? Run against me? A disgraced cop? Get real." Jules stood up before he did. And when Mayor Windbreeze did, the room became deathly quiet. "You will not run against me. I have things just the way I like them. You might think that you can do the job, but we both know that you would fuck it up worse than I have."

"You think so, do you?" Jules turned to Christian. "I'm doing it. Fix up whatever you need for me to run, and I'll go and talk to Levi."

Jules, now that he hadn't gotten upset at being called that, started out the door, but returned. Pushing Windbag into his chair again, he leaned over him so that his face was just an inch from his. Then he let his cat take him. It was the scariest thing Christian had ever seen his brother do. When he shifted back, he was dressed, something that he'd not thought would happen to him. He figured Dane was spreading her blood around for them all for him to be able to do that.

"Fuck with me and I'll take you down right now.

Understand me? I was not a disgraced cop. You yourself pinned several medals of honor on my chest when I went above and beyond the call of duty. You call me that again, and I will rip out your tongue and hang you with it."

When he snapped his teeth at him, Christian stood very still until he was gone again. The smell of piss permeated the room.

"He just threatened me. Did you see that?" Christian said nothing. "He said he was going to kill me. Made himself into a large cougar and threatened me with him."

"Actually, he didn't." The mayor stood up, then sat again when Christian looked at his pants. "He said he'd rip your tongue out and hang you with it. His cat can't do that. And even with that, I don't think it was a threat at all, but a promise. You'd do well to remember that. And when I send you the cleaning bill, you had better not return it. You do, and I'll have the cameras that were on you when you entered hit the airway, and you'll be the laughing stock of the town. More so then you are now."

After Windbag left, Christian pulled out the charter on being mayor. Just the first paragraph of rules was being broken in that the mayor had to attend seven meetings a month that the mayor was supposed to have set up. Not to mention, there was a rider in there that he was to head several committees that would make at least one improvement, or be in the works of an improvement, per year. He'd been in office for four years, and not one thing was finished that Christian's family hadn't taken over recently. Christian called his dad.

"Jules is running for mayor." The quickest and most efficient way to get the word out was to tell his dad. He'd never break a secret, but he would tell everyone around something that was soon to be public knowledge. Christian took the phone from his ear when his dad yelled. When he put it back to listen, he could hear his dad telling whoever he was with the news. "I need you to help him get the word out."

"You bet your bottom dollar I will. Tell me his plan." He said that he'd only just decided, then he told him about what had happened in his office. "I think this will be just what he needs. He's been sluggish around the house. Well, not sluggish, but something was wrong with him. I'll go over and see Levi now. I'm betting that he can get him started on something. Thanks for calling me, Christian. By the way, did you know that he's going by Jules now?"

"I did. He told me the other night that Tess calls him that, and it doesn't bother him anymore." They had all, except Wyatt and Levi, had names that could have been shortened, but they'd not done it. Brayden *wouldn't* do it, not after the experience he had with someone calling him Brady all the time. "Anyway, you meet up with him at Levi's office and we'll go from there."

Christian started making notes, not just on what Windbag wasn't doing, but what needed to be done. By the time lunch was coming around, he had a list of about twenty-three things that should have been taken care of, as well as a longer list of things that needed to be taken care of very soon. Then there was the list, which most of the things were on and that he'd marked immediately, that were already being taken care of by his family in different ways. The grand opening of the veterans/handicapped workout house being the big one. Christian called his mom.

"When does your next women's thing meet?" Mom said tomorrow. "I don't think that's enough time. I need for you to work with me on something."

"Does this have to do with Jules running for mayor?" Laughing, he told her that it did. "Then there is plenty of time. Tell me what you need."

"I was thinking that we need a clothing drive. There is supposed to be one done twice a year by the mayor. If we can get Jules to head one up, say next weekend, he can announce to the public that he's going to be running against Windbag." She laughed at the nickname. "I wish I had come up with it, but Jules calls him that. And apparently for a long time too."

"I love it. And I love the clothing drive as well. Oh my yes. Cleaning out the closets before spring is in full bloom. Yes, I'll make some calls. Also, last month we were thinking of one of those handy-bags—toothpaste and brushes, with a little bit of things like deodorant for the young teenagers. Some of them need to have it, but I don't think they realize it yet. That's what we were going to do."

"Why can't we combine the things? Get the kids to help us out." Mom was as excited sounding as he was getting. "Jules can be there with his new wife and daughter. Make an afternoon of it. Then when the kids are finished up, we feed them pizza."

"Oh, I love that very much. All right, I need to get calling." His mom came back on the line by saying his name. "Windbag, has he heard about this?"

"Yes, he has, and as you can imagine, he's not all that happy about it either."

They were both laughing hard when they disconnected

the call. He wasn't worried about Mom not coming through for them. What concerned him was how overboard the drives were going to be. When his mom spoke, people listened.

Chapter 5

Tess was careful with counting every item that she used during surgery. But this was a new hospital for her, and she didn't want to step on toes. As she was counting them in her head, Granddad, still in his cast, told her to do it. It was what she did, and they'd have to get used to it. So she had the surgery nurse dump out the bag that she'd put them in and count them twice. There was one missing.

"I could have sworn they were all in here." The entire room dropped what they were doing to look for the last sponge. Finally it was found near the bed under the shoe of a nurse. After that, she told them that it was her job to make sure that it was all accounted for, and thanked the nurse for counting again. "You're very welcome. And I must say, Dr. Stanton, it's a real pleasure to work with you."

They were set to be married this evening in a big way. The plan had been to just let the one they had stand, but since Jules was running for the mayor position, she was sure it was to get votes. It didn't matter to her why, but she was glad to have it for Lucy. She loved that woman as much as she'd loved her grandma when she'd been alive. And today was the big day.

"You ready?" She asked Granddad what he meant. "You've not heard then? I'm sorry. I would have thought that Jules would have talked to you about it."

"I've asked him not to talk to me during surgeries. I don't want to lose my concentration. And I've not let him know that I'm finished. What's happened?" Granddad told her. "That's wonderful. Jules is going to love going to those meetings. I wish I could go with him."

"You are, honey. It's the day after you get back. I thought you'd be upset with him being out in the public eye. You do understand that that means you'll have to be out there too." She told Granddad that whatever made Jules happy, it thrilled her to death. "I'm glad to hear that. I think he'll make a fine mayor, don't you?"

"I do. He's been kind of bored with himself. And if he wakes up Ruby from her nap again, I'm going to brain him. He'll poke at her when he's nothing to do so that she can play with him. Makes for a hard bedtime." Granddad laughed. "You wouldn't think it was so funny if you saw how upset she is. And you should see him with her, Granddad. He gives her a bath and spends all his time helping her with walking. He loves her better than I ever thought a man could."

"Of course he loves her. And you too." She flushed a little bit. "You and him, you're going to have more, aren't you? I'd love another grandchild or two."

"I've heard that you're going to be great granddad to all

the Stantons' children. So, you cannot be begging me for them when I know that you have at least two more coming along soon." He laughed with her. "Now, I have to have a meeting with the head of surgery. You coming with me?"

"He asked me to come along. Is that all right with you?" She told him she was glad to have him. "I have an idea that he's going to ask you to stay on here. I know that you were working for me, but you've done a fine job of it. I'm betting he asks."

"I was worried he was going to tell me the opposite. You know, we've read over your records and you're too bossy or too in debt." He asked if he could please take care of it for her. "Jules already did it. He told me last night. I have to be honest with you, Granddad, I've never loved anyone like I do him. And he's so kind to me. Just...he's just kind to me."

"You deserve it more than most, I think." He walked with her down the hall. "What's your plans after you're married? I noticed that the staff calls you Dr. Stanton already. Nothing like keeping it in the family. I love it, by the way."

Today she'd be married at the big house that Jules had grown up in. And his parents were going to keep an eye on Ruby while they spent the next two days in Columbus, Ohio. Then in a few months, after Ruby was a little older and maybe walking, in the warmer weather, they'd take a longer vacation where there was a beach.

It was the honeymoon she was looking forward to. She's been shopping online, had herself some pretty things to wear and something nice to wear for dinner out. But right now, she had to think about what she was doing in the office of the head of surgery. Her granddad kissed her on the cheek and told her to go get him. This was going to be bad, she knew it.

"Hello, Dr. Stanton, Dr. O'Rourke. I hope that we can be a little informal here." They both said it was all right with them and told him their first names. "I'm David Craven. And you may or may not have heard, but I'm not the sort to beat around the bush. I'm retiring in a few weeks, on my seventieth birthday as a matter of fact. And I'd like for you, Tess, to take my job. I'd have offered it to your grandfather, but he told me that he's retiring as well."

"Granddad?" He told her that he was having too much fun hanging out with friends and playing with Ruby. "I don't know what to say. I thought for sure that you'd just want me to not come around anymore."

"Not come around? My goodness, girl. Kendal Wayne is home now, feeling better than he has in years, I've heard. He has a good job, his wife is working too, and that is thanks to you. You saved that man's life. Because as surely as we're sitting here, I don't think he might have lived long with the pain of it." She shook her head. "He told me that himself, honey. You saved him and his wife's lives. She would have joined him."

Tess had a lot to learn about shifters, apparently, but right now she had a decision to make. He was telling her about the hours, which weren't too bad, the pay, and what her perks would be. The perks alone would save her a great deal of money with children in the house. No medical cost to her at all, or her family.

"I'll have to talk it over with Jules." He laughed and told her that he heard he was running for mayor next term. "Yes, I think he'll do an amazing job, don't you?"

70

"I brought that little boy into this world, him and his brothers. There is not a better family around than the Stantons. I'm so happy that you're in their family. I have to admit, Dane frightens me a bit, and so does that Allie. That girl has moves that makes me think she has no bones." They laughed. "You take a couple of days and let—"

"I'll take it." She laughed at herself. "I'm sure that Jules will support me, and this is just what I've wanted all my career. But we're getting married tonight—you'll be there, correct?—anyway, we'll need some time off for that."

"Vacations are a part of your package, and a signing bonus as well. The hospital also said that if you took the job, they'd give you all the advertising money they were going to spend on luring someone here to take it. You've saved me a lot of time too. I hate to interview people."

When she was walking out a bit later, she realized that she had a job. Staggering just a little, she was making her way to the elevator when her granddad touched her face with his hands.

"Are you awake now?" She nodded. "You walked out on him. I think he wanted you to see your new office. He said that it's down the hall here."

Tess followed him while reaching out to Jules. He had bitten her a few days ago so that they could talk. But she was waiting on them making love. Sex was all she'd been able to think about since he'd kissed her.

Congratulations, my dear. Chief of surgery. What are you going to do with such a prestigious title? We'll be Mayor and Doctor Stanton. Christ, that sound pretentious. She asked him why she had to be second. *Oh, I'm so sorry. We'll be Doctor and*

Mr. Mayor. That better for you? By the way, I hope you don't mind, but I turned down the house that came with it if I get it. That way we don't have to start over. You think I have a chance?

You're hands down going to be the mayor if the people in my operating room have any say in it. And I think that Doctor Craven might vote for you too because I helped him retire. They talked a little more, at least until she entered her office. *Oh Jules, it's beautiful. Empty, but very pretty. I can see our house from here. As well as the main street. How beautiful.*

We have a desk that you can have. But I'm thinking you need something huge and newer. I'll have to help you look around. She told him she wanted her granddad's old desk, or one like it if he didn't want to get rid of it. *Oh honey, that's a great idea. And Dad, he'll be thrilled to death to have you there. He'll have a million and one ideas for you, too, to make improvements. He's been wanting a new wing for the children's area for years. He'd more than likely do that for you.*

The Dexter and Alma Shipley Children's Ward. She had no idea why that popped into her head, but that was what she was going to suggest they name it. If they allowed her to do so. As she looked around the office, Granddad made notes — the size of the room, the door size, as well as the walls. Before this was done, he would be able to tell her if a shelf that she was looking at would not just fit on the wall, but through the door as well.

"You should take that old desk of mine." She looked at him with a smile. "Your grandma bought me that when I first started out as a doctor in college. She'd love for you to have it."

"I was trying to think how I should ask you for it. Do you

72

think it would fit through the door?" He said that it would. "Then yes, I'll take it. And I also want a shelf that Lucy showed me the other day that is in the barn. I want to clean that up and put it here for pictures."

Her licenses were in storage—she'd been terrified that someone, Dexter, would get in and get to them—but she knew that he wasn't being destructive, but he was sick. She had so loved him as a child, and to see him this way, suffering the way he was, it hurt her deeply.

The rest of the day was spent with her getting ready. There was a spa day that she was both looking forward to and not. She didn't like to have anyone messing with her feet, but when she'd told the woman, she had whipped out a large stone and began scrubbing all the dead skin away. After showing her what two minutes of work looked like, she was happy to have her feet touched. And she was ready for her hands to be done as well.

As a surgeon, she never had nice long nails. She had this fear of the germs that were usually under them, and had decided early on in her career never to have them any longer than her tips. But to have them buffed and painted now, she thought she could get used to this. Having herself pampered was sort of fun.

"Your hair, have you decided what to do with it?"

She said that she was just going to wear one of her old dresses with her hair pulled up in a nice bun. Lucy laughed and said that she wasn't. As she was taken to the back room of the shop, she almost messed up her face, as the woman who had done her makeup had called it, when she saw her grandmother's dress hanging on a soft silk hanger.

"Ericson said that your mother wore it as well." Crying at the beauty of it, she nodded at Lucy. "We've had it cleaned and repaired, just some lace that needed a stitch or two. And Mabel is going to fit it for you. Though now that I see it, I'm betting that it fits you like a glove."

It did. Not only did it fit her, but with a photo of her mom and grandmother, she was able to have her hair styled the same way — a long braid down the back, with pinned pearls in it. Then it was wrapped up around her head for the veil.

"That's not all we've done for you either, my dear. Look at dear little Ruby." Ruby had been playing in a walker for the last few days. She didn't get far, but she could move in circles. The little boy that was pushing her was gentle with her, and brought her right to her. "Look at her dress, honey."

Pulling her out of the little walker, she held her little girl out and looked at her dress. It was as ruby red as her name, and her shoes looked like the slippers from the movie with the witch. Her baby looked so happy to be all dressed up. And her hair, usually a mess, was moosed back into curls, and she had a little tiara on.

This time there was no stopping the tears. "Lucy, you've done so much for me. I just don't know what to say." She told her it was her first wedding of her sons, since the others had gotten married in the courthouse, and that she was enjoying it. "But Ruby, what you did for her is amazing."

"You should see the design that we're coming up with for the walker. Brayden has gone all out. And he's having a blast too. And you having me be your matron of honor — you have no idea how wonderful you've made me feel." She told her about the office and her new job. "Well, that shelf you wanted, it'll be perfect. I'll have one of the boys take it out to have it cleaned up. Oh my, what a wonderful day this is turning out to be."

By the time she was dressed, the walker was complete. Ruby had had a nap, so she'd be in a much better mood, and Tess had on her grandmother's dress. Lucy was right, it was turning out to be a wonderful day.

~~~

Jules helped his dad with his tie. There were only a few people here, he knew that, but he was still nervous. His dad seemed to be as well. When he asked him for the hundredth time what was going on, he finally broke.

"Your wife, she's a beauty." He said that he knew that too. "Well, I have to tell you something that I'm so afraid of messing up. I've never been a granddaddy before. I mean, I've thought of nothing else since we found out about the other two babies coming along, but now she's here. Little Ruby, she's my first grandbaby, and I'm afraid of hurting her."

"Dad, I don't think you could ever hurt anyone." He said that wasn't what he meant. "Then tell me. That kid loves you. She just brightens up every time she sees you."

"I mean, I might be hurting us by being too strict. I can't do it, Jules. I have thought it over, and I want to be a granddad, not a man who she avoids because she can't wrap me around her finger. And you know what? I don't think I'm going to be all that good at that anyway." He asked him who had said he had to be that way. "I don't want her coming to me when you tell her no. Well, I do, but I don't want to cause any trouble between us because I give in to her."

"I want you to give in to her. Not on everything. We have

to have rules. But you're going to be her grandfather, and I remember my own grandmother. She wasn't at all like what you're describing. We were terrified of her." He said that he'd been afraid of his mom too. "She was just so sour. I'll tell you something, Dad; we used to pretend to be sick, so we'd not have to go there as much. I know that's horrible, but she never made us feel very welcome."

"I'm sorry about that. I am. And your mom and I, we had that figured out anyway. I was a doctor, you know." They both laughed. "I'll be careful not to touch on things that we shouldn't be giving into. I promise you that. But I would like to take her all night too. And to take her and the others on trips with us. My goodness, your mother and I have been looking at large vans, so we can take them on long trips with us."

"It's a deal. With our business schedule, we're hiring a nanny for her. I know that you'll babysit anytime we want you to, but this will be too much for you. Even for us, I think. And I don't want you and Mom worn out too much when you want to take her out." He laughed. "Dad, I want you to have her anytime you want. And you won't want to when you've had her entirely too much, because of babysitting."

"I like that idea. And a nanny you can trust too." Jules told him that was their number one priority." Good, good. You're having Dane help you out with that, I'm betting."

"Yes. I don't think she'd let us do it any other way." They were both laughing when the music started. It was time for them to go out and wait on his bride to be. "Dad, thanks for being my best man. And for Mom helping with everything too."

"Our pleasure."

They went out to stand where they were supposed to, and he was glad now that they'd decided to have the wedding at his parents' house. Dad was going to be doing a lot of duties here today, and he was happy that he had them around. Ruby could not be in better hands today, and for the rest of the weekend.

His mom came out in front of the flower girl. And when the little motorized walker came out, he saw that Brayden had done it up really nice. There were flowers everywhere on it, as well as a little bowl of fruit for Ruby to eat if she was bored. The way she was flying up and down the little walkway, she was screaming at the top of her lungs with glee. He was glad that someone was recording her fun. He couldn't wait to show it to her when she was a little older.

Next came his bride. To say that she was beautiful would have been a gross understatement. She was whatever word surpassed beautiful. She was gorgeous, stunning, and his. Everything about her screamed lovely, from the veil on top of her head to the bottom of her jewel encased feet.

The dress was a lovely shade of ivory. Seed pearls, what his mom had called them, were all over the lower half of the dress. The sleeves were lace, covering her from wrist to breasts, and then down the other side of her body. He had never seen a more beautiful gown. And he was sure it had to do with the woman wearing it.

They had decided not to have flowers in the event that she'd have to hold Ruby when this started, so Tess held a small white Bible that had been her mother's. When she needed to store it, he could put it in his own jacket pocket, and then it wouldn't be lost. As soon as she was near him, he pulled the veil over her head and kissed her like a man starved.

The room erupted in a chorus of cheers. It was funny, really, the way the clergy cleared his throat and told him to behave. He thought he was. Jules hadn't thrown her to the floor yet and taken her. That was what he really wanted to do.

When he and Tess were pronounced man and wife, he took Ruby from Tess. He held her to his heart as she patted him on the back and laid her head to his shoulder. He turned to the family that was there and the few friends that they had invited.

"Today I took this little girl's mom to my heart, gave her my name, and will worship her for the rest of her days. Tess Stanton is the best thing that has ever happened to me. And in that wonderful gift of love, I gained a daughter. Ruby Denise Stanton is now and forever my daughter. Not because the paperwork says that she is, but because in my heart she belongs there. She is my child. I will never treat her any differently if she is not our only daughter. I will never disrespect her by saying that she's not my biological child. As far as I'm concerned, there was no other male in her life but me, and I will love her forever because her mom gave her to me." When he kissed her on the mouth, Ruby said as clear as day, "Da Da." Jules felt like a man blessed at that very moment.

Dinner was served after the service. Mostly it was just sandwiches — that was what Tess had wanted. It was easiest to make, clean up, and to store leftovers. There was also a mountain of fruit and vegetables, and dips. When the last guest was served, he and Tess slipped out the back and to their hotel.

Jules had been planning all day for tonight. Hell, he thought, he'd been planning this for his entire life, it felt like. A wife needed special, and he'd been on the Internet for several hours every day to get this just right. There was chocolate and strawberries, champagne and diamonds, and he had roses and more roses for her.

While she was changing, he prepared the rest of the things he'd gotten her. The berries were fresh, the wine chilled. He poured them both a glass when he heard the door open, and turned around and simply crushed the glasses in his hands. He had expected a nightie, but what he got was so much less.

"I forgot to pack my pretty nightie." He nodded, unable to speak. Jules wasn't even sure that he could breathe again. "So I thought, what the heck, I'll just be naked. That's what we want anyway, correct?"

"Yes. That's what I want. You're more beautiful than I ever thought possible." She came to him, walking on heels that made her legs look a mile long. "Turn around. I want to see all of you."

She did, standing on the heels like she'd been born to them. And when she was facing him again, she cupped her breasts in her hands and moaned. She was, he knew, going to kill him before the night was through.

"I've thought of nothing else but having you make love to me." He nodded, and she giggled. "You've cut your hands, love. Do you want me to kiss them and make it all better?"

"Yes. You can kiss all of me, if you wish." She said that she would. As she unfastened his tie, he wiped the blood, really very little of it considering that he'd broken two glasses, onto the towel. Before he could figure out her intentions, she was on the floor in front of him taking his belt off. "I want you."

"And I'm yours. But for now, I want to see you. You've seen all of me, haven't you?" He nodded as she unbuttoned his pants. "I love the sound of your zipper when it goes down for me. It's like the sound a race car makes when it's revving up."

When he was freed from his pants and boxers, he reached out to fist his cock. But she took him deep into her mouth and he cried out. Christ, she really was going to have him die on their wedding night. As soon as she swallowed him past the tight muscles at the back of her throat, he came so hard he had to hold onto her before he fell.

"My turn." She told him she wasn't finished. "Oh, but you are for now. It's my turn. I want to taste you, lick your pussy until you fill my mouth with your come. I want to feel you tighten around my cock when I'm deep inside of you."

Helping her to stand, he picked her up in his arms. Instead of laying her on the bed, as was his intention, he suckled at her breast and then laid her down. As soon as she was comfy in the middle, he joined her on the bed between her thighs. Jules needed her. Without telling her what he wanted, he dove into her pussy like he was getting his last meal, breakfast, lunch, and dinner, as well as dessert. She came three times before he was finished. Or just getting started, however one wanted to look at it.

"Now to make love to you." He laid by her, his body hard with need. But he wanted her to have as much pleasure as he could give her.

Touching her breasts with his fingers, he licked the tight buds. Then when she moaned, he blew warm air over them, to see them tighten more. Her belly was smooth, and her navel was pierced. He loved that about her, and laved her navel indentation with his tongue over and over.

As soon as he entered her, she came hard. Jules made love to her slowly, bringing her over and over until she was limp in his arms. When she lifted her legs up, wrapping them around his hips, he took her quickly then, deepening each stroke until he released. And what a glorious climax it was.

Jules leaned into her neck when she offered it to him. Biting gently at first, the warm blood made him realize that she was in heat. Not asking her—it was too late by then—he took her harder, his body knowing, as well as his cat did, that they were making a child tonight. When he came again he bit her harder, drawing a scream from her, but she also bit deeply into his throat too. They were married. They were a family.

"I'm pregnant now, I think." He lifted his head up and looked at her. "I'm a doctor, Jules. And I know the signs too."

"Well, that took the thunder out of my storm." As she was giggling again, he pulled her over him when he rolled to his back. "I'm so happy right now, love. Another baby. I can't believe our luck."

"Did you mean what you said, about Ruby?" Jules said he meant every word he said today. "Good. She's going to love having a family too. I know that I am. Now, leave me be, you've worn me out. And when I wake you later, you'd better be ready. I'm not finished with you yet."

When she rolled to her side, he laid there. Christ, his wife, his very own wife, was going to jump his bones. Rolling to his own side, curling up behind her, Jules thought that he wouldn't have it any other way. And she could jump his bones whenever she wanted.

Chapter 6

Taking in the sites meant so much more than they had before. Tess loved the way that Jules took pride in the state's capitol. They even had lunch at one of his favorite restaurants while there. And then they made a stop at the North Market and bought all kinds of things, making two trips to the car before calling it a day and heading home. And through it all, they loved, kissed, and touched one another whenever they could.

"I need my little girl." He laughed when she explained why. "I've never gone this long without nursing her. And I know that I've pumped them, but they still feel full. And no, you can't help me out again. While that was fun, I don't think your daughter will like it if you're as greedy as she is."

The pouty lip nearly got her laughing at him. "You know you loved it as much as I did." She had, and was embarrassed at how much she had. "Anyway, Mom and Dad are going to bring her over to our house as soon as we get there. You can feed her until she pops."

She hadn't really missed her daughter until now. They had spent a lot of money on getting Ruby fun things, also a few things for her room. Her room was perfect, but she didn't have any clothing that was hers. They both wanted her to have that. Also, while the room was finished up, it was cold looking—nothing personal in the room. Nor were there any little books or stuffed dolls. That was something that she wanted her to have. Warmth in the room she was going to call her own.

They had also talked about Dexter while they had been away. It gave them distance from him, not just in miles, but in knowing that they were somehow safe too. But he wasn't, and they both knew it.

"I just heard from Dane. She said to let you know that he took the twenty dollars out of the account she put in there for you. And that he took it surprisingly well that you no longer have an account there. What do you suppose he's thinking now?" Lots of things ran through her mind, none of them very good. "We're doing the best we can in not allowing him to be hurt, Tess. You know that, don't you? Whatever happened in that house, it sent a reasonably sane man over the edge."

"We know that she killed the girl and the little boy. What will happen with that? I mean, there won't be any justice served." He told her that there would be, and how. "Really? They'll have a trial for a dead woman? Why?"

"For one thing, there are the insurance policies. Someone will have to collect on them, and without a cause of death, in this case being murder, there might be more money coming. And since she wasn't married to Dexter, her parents will get it. Any justice that comes from the death of the child, that will be his. He might need it while he's recovering from all this." She asked him if he thought he would. "Yes. I have to believe that, or there isn't any point in trying to make it work for him. I believe that we can bring him around. It's something that we have to do or we'll lose him. And I don't want that to happen any more than you do. What his state of mind will be afterwards, I don't know, but I do know that with help, he'll understand better."

She nodded and thought of Dexter the last few months. "When the two of us would see each other, it was the strangest thing. I mean, I noticed it before, but now, with the knowledge that I have presently, I understand what he was doing." Jules asked her what she meant. "He was forever looking around. I thought that he was trying to escape being with me, but I think he was searching for his mom. She never liked me, as I said, and she would have been harder on him seeing that we were together. Do you suppose that she made him suffer somehow for that? Being with me? I wonder if she knew that I was marrying Kenneth so that he could stay with Daniel. Not that it would have been any of her business, but I wonder what she would have thought of me living with a gay couple. I have all kinds of questions going through my head, but without any answers. There might not ever be any if he doesn't get better."

"Why did you do that? Agree to marry Kenneth, if you don't mind me asking. I mean, it doesn't seem like you needed them to protect you, did you? Not then." She told him she wanted to pay off her student loans with the money they had paid her to have a child for them. "I see. And then when he was killed, it was too much on the other. Not that I mind you being left with Ruby, but I did wonder."

So many things about their life was becoming clearer. Not just hers, but Dexter's too. The times when they were children were difficult to think about at times, but she had thought back then it was because he was an awkward kid—him being so much smarter than her. When all along it was just his mom. She wondered about other things too.

"Did Debra mention me in the books?" He said he knew that Dane said that she had, but he didn't know what she'd said. "I would have thought plenty. Dexter was the first boy I kissed. We were about eleven then. Anyway, his mom caught us. She beat us both bloody over that. My grandma took a switch to her when she found out. I don't remember the details, but I know that Debra wasn't allowed to be around me anymore. Which was fine by me. The kiss wasn't even all that much—I touched my mouth to his cheek, that's it. But she freaked out like we were having sex right there in the yard. I was so hurt over that; she called me a whore. And I had to ask Grandma what that meant."

"The firm that he worked for, they thought he was a homosexual because he was so backward around women that they thought that was the reason. And as far as anyone knew, he never dated either. That's the reason they were so shocked to hear that he had, first of all, a fiancée, and then a living mother. The funny part about that is, Dexter sent her money every month, and she took it. We know that she deposited the money into her account, and that she used it too. But no one ever knew that she was a person until he asked for the time off." Tess nodded. "When you were younger, did you ever see any men around?"

"No, why? Is that important?" He said that Dane had asked him to ask her. "There was an uncle, a real uncle, that came around once in a great while, but even that stopped after the beat down with me. I'm not sure there was anyone else. I think I read someplace that he was dead too. I don't think she had anything to do with it, but knowing her, I wouldn't put it past her."

"She didn't know she was going to have a baby, we mentioned that before. Wyatt and Colton got together, and they have an idea that she thinks her baby was a gift from God. She thinks somehow that Dexter might have been the second coming of Christ. There is mention in the books that she kept that he was conceived by that method. But that wasn't until later in the books, about the time he turned five or so." She stared at him, not sure what to think. "There is mention of him being godly. They're not sure what that might mean, but the more they read about him and his birth, that's what they think. And Dane is going to go to your grade school, as well as other places that he went to school, to get some insight on him. Someone there is bound to remember someone like him. Backward, odd mother, not to mention, from what they've gathered, he was a slob in the way he dressed. He might not have had much."

"That is so sad. I mean, she had to have had sex. So why would she think something like that?" Jules explained that she was older when she had him. "Yes, I do remember that. She was at least twenty years older than my parents. Or she seemed older. I don't know anymore. But when he suddenly appeared on the scene, as my mom called it, there was some speculation that he'd been stolen or something. I'm not sure."

They were pulling into the drive when something else occurred to her. She wondered where Debra was getting money besides what she was getting from Dexter since she'd lost her job with the bank. What he sent couldn't have been enough to pay bills, taxes, and a house payment, could it? And what sort of pension, if any, did she have? Houses in their neighborhood weren't like the Stanton homes, but they were well kept. Who mowed the lawn or shoveled the drive and such? These were not things that Debra would have done on her own. She just knew that Dane would know the answer and was happy to find her at their house when they arrived.

"She had a pension, as you might have guessed. Not much, but the house was her parents', and all she needed to do was to keep up with the taxes. She did that, but not well, not until she had help from Dexter. Though why he'd help her is beyond me. And we think that Dexter might have helped her with repairs, too. There were uncashed checks, not many of them, within the diaries that she wrote in. Devil's money she called it, because it wasn't really cash." Dane handed her some photos. "I found these. There weren't many pictures of anyone in the house when we went there. But I don't suppose you can help us with who these people might be."

"This is my older brother. He passed away when I was a teenager. He was in a car accident that took my father's life too. When it was obvious that he wasn't going to be better, my mom did something that few could have. Then a week later, she died as well. Alex had severe brain damage, and I think, somehow, she thought it was her fault that he died and ended her own life." She looked at the picture closer. "That's me in the red jumper. I don't know who this little boy is, and that's Dexter. My goodness, were we ever that young?"

"The little boy is a kid by the name of Davie; does that ring a bell?" She said yes, but not that she could place him. "Davie's parents were interracial. It wasn't as common as it is now, but they moved away almost a year after purchasing their first home. They basically forfeited everything they owned to get away from Debra. She made their lives a living hell. And then one night she burned a cross in their front yard."

"There are others, too. Aren't there? Other people that she terrorized." Dane nodded. "Why? Other than she was a mean bitch, what could have led her to believe she could be like this to people?"

"All in the name of God. She actually believed that Dexter was the son of God. Or a god. It wasn't clear to her who he might have been fathered by. And before you ask, no, we don't think she had more than one lover. But we have found enough evidence around the house to positively identify his father." Tess asked why that was important. "We've unearthed a few more bodies than just Alma and her son. They're pretty close to what was at one time an outhouse. I don't know when it was torn down, but I think it was the place she put people that pissed her off, because the ground was softer there. I don't want to think that there might have been any other reason."

"I wouldn't put anything past her. She wasn't nice; she had no reason to be like she was. Dexter was a nice kid, smart beyond compare, and he never, so far as I know, ever caused any trouble. After I moved in with my grandparents, neighbor to Dexter, I realized that she was the meanest woman I'd ever met. And then some." Dane asked where she'd known Dexter from before. "We went to school together. He was in a higher grade, but we were the same age."

~~~

After they all left, Tess went to the library that Jules had set up first thing. When he asked if she needed him to join her, she asked him to keep an eye on Ruby for a little while, that she needed to think. He didn't like leaving her alone right now, but he knew that she was a thinker and did better when alone. So, when Ruby woke from her nap, after Mommy fed her he took her to the backyard to play.

It was a warm day today, and while winter was still hanging on, he could see buds on some of the heartier trees, as well as some bulbs coming up. Last fall he'd marked all the ones that he'd wanted transplanted, and was excited to see what was going to be coming up.

Just as he was going to pick a small bloom for Ruby to smell, he saw Dexter. He was hiding, but not well. More like he wasn't hiding from him, but whoever was behind him. That was the direction that he kept looking in. Whatever he was doing here, he was reasonably sure that he was not hiding from him, but from someone else. When his brother came out of the woods beside him, Jules reached out to Levi and let him know not to startle him.

I knew he was there, but I didn't want you to think we weren't watching out for you guys. Dexter has been in the woods for over an hour, I guess. I don't know who he's hiding from, but he will drop down and lay under the leaves for a few minutes every time he hears something. There isn't anyone here but us. Jules told him he'd thought the same thing. *I'll keep an eye on him. Watch out for Ruby.*

90

When Dexter suddenly came running toward him, he picked the baby up, ready to run into the house if need be. But all he did was stand about a foot from him and look around, speaking softly.

"Don't let her see her." He told Dexter that he'd not. "She'll kill her, the baby I mean. Not Tessie, not unless she gets in her way. Mom is all wrong in the head. No kids. No kids. No kids."

"Dexter, are you all right?" He said that he needed him to watch for Tessie too. To keep her away from him. "Dexter, why don't you come with me? Perhaps we can do something to help you out."

He'd been told not to mention Alma or the baby. Dexter said no kids a dozen more times before Tess came out and took Ruby from Jules, but didn't leave. And just like that, he could see the clarity in Dexter's eyes. The man was in love with her. But as Tess had said, not in love like a man loves a woman, but more like a big brother or something. She held her little girl now, but Jules was no less vigilant about keeping them safe.

"Hello Tessie. Your little girl is very pretty. So are you."

Tess thanked him and smiled. When he started to cry, Jules was given Ruby, and he then handed her to the nanny. When she was clear of the area, he looked at Tessie holding Dexter.

"I'm so confused. There was so much blood and stuff. I don't know where I was hurt either. Then she was gone. I can see her face, but not like it was before. Now she's gone, and I can't remember who she is. Do you?"

"No, I'm sorry, I don't know. But it's all right, Dex. You let me take care of you. You need help, don't you? You want me to help you, Dex?" He stiffened and looked at her. "Dexter?"

"Whore. You whore." When he drew back to hit her, Jules moved to cut him off. "She's a slut, and I don't want her around my son. Do you hear me? Throwing herself at him like the tart that she is. You keep that child of yours away from him. He's god's child, and he's pure."

"They were only talking. Why do you think she's a whore, Debra?" Jules knew that he was looking at her now, Dexter's mother, and that frightened him on a great many levels. "Why don't you allow me to talk to Dexter again? He—"

"You leave him alone. Do you hear me? He's mine, and I will not have you making him believe things that you do. Whore." She looked at the house, then back at him. "I've told him over and over and over. No kids. I want no kids. No kids, no kids, no kids."

When Dexter/Debra walked away, Jules wasn't sure what had just happened, but he did know that he had to talk to his brothers. And his dad. When Tess came to him, her arms wrapped tightly around him, he reached out to his family, all of them, to tell them what had just happened.

That's just what we thought. He's both of them. And as much as I hate to say this, I think he might have been doing this all along.

Jules wasn't sure, but he thought he might be right on that.

But if that's true, how can we help him? How indeed, he wanted to say, but didn't when Tess continued. *Where will he go now that he knows that I'm staying here? He even acknowledged Ruby and how pretty she is. Then his mom came there too, didn't she? Even when you called her by her name, she didn't even flinch.*

He's really himself and his mom.

I'd say that's about it. But there are still things that we can do. Especially since we know now that he's both of them. Don't leave Ruby out where he can see her again. Jules promised that they'd keep her safe. Colton told them he wanted to look into some things before he had an answer. *And when I get the answers that I need, I'm thinking that we might not care for the answers. Just so that you're aware of it.*

Jules wasn't sure that Tess should be around him at all. Not even when it was just Dexter. But they did need to get him help, and this was the best way. He supposed. What did he know? He was just a retired beat cop trying to be mayor of this town.

~~~

"But Mom, I don't know where she might be living. I told you, I just happened upon them." Dexter's head was pounding again. He was sick with it. And he just wanted to sleep. But Mom was mad at him again, and he was trying to get her to be quiet so that he could rest his head. "Mom? Did you leave me?"

He hoped so. There was something there, something that he couldn't touch about his mom. A memory or a thought. Something that she'd done. And when he was having one of his blackouts, he knew it was because of her. She'd hit him, or something worse.

Then he felt it, felt her there close. But he never saw her anymore. Feeling her was bad enough. He wasn't sure that he wanted to see her.

"No, I did not leave you. I'm right here. Why are you forever asking me that? Can you not see me?" She huffed, a sure sign that

she was unhappy with him. *"Dexter, I have told you a thousand times to stop hanging out with that girl. You have nothing in common with her. As the son of God, you must be better at picking your friends. And since she's some whore with a child, you have to make sure that the child is taken care of. Bring her to me. I will make sure that she's...I'll make sure that it's taken care of."*

"I like her. And the little baby. She's pretty, like Tessie is. And her name is Ruby, not it. I don't want you to take her someplace." He knew she was upset, knew that it was only a matter of time before she hit him again. Like she had when he was just a child. He waited for the sting of her hand, but it didn't come. "Mom, when can I go home again? I don't like it here."

This was his house, on some level he knew that, but he didn't like this place anymore. There were rooms here that he couldn't open. Picture frames that had no picture in them. There were other things too, too many towels for just him. The bed was too big, and there were things in his room that smelled pretty that gave him a headache. And if he tried to open the door to one of the rooms, his head would feel like it was ready to split open and he'd have to throw up. Again and again.

"No, you can't go there. I'm having the walls cleaned and painted." That was what she said every time he brought it up. *"Besides, you don't want to go there without me, do you? That's my house, and you are to stay out of it. But let's talk about this man, the one that was holding that little baby. What have I told you about children, Dexter? What?"*

"No kids. No kids. No kids." She told him that was right, but when he thought about that, something in his head hurt badly. He didn't understand his head. Before...before something had happened, he never had headaches. Blood. There was—

"Dexter, you're going to make me upset with you if you don't start saying it and believing in it. You are the son of God. You must believe me when I tell you that you cannot have children. They're made in sin. I didn't sin, and look, I have you. So you keep saying that. Say it Dexter, now."

"No kids. No kids. No kids." His mind was working while his mouth was busy. But whenever he tried to think about what was there, just on the edge of his mind, it would skitter away like a bug on a hot light. "Mom? Where is he?"

"He who? Who is it you're forever asking me about?" He didn't know and told her that. But the room was all red and moving around. *"Then how do you expect me to tell you where he is if you don't tell me who he is?"*

"Yes, of course." He kept saying the words over and over. But the pain in his head had him leaning over and puking. Laying his head back down on the couch, he held the trash can to him. "I don't feel well again."

He knew that he'd not eaten in days. His clothing no longer fit him. Even his shoes seemed to be about a size too large for him. Throwing up no longer brought up the green bile, but now he was puking up blood. Dexter didn't want to think what he might have hurt when he was sick like this.

Seeing the blood made him close his eyes. That was another thing that bothered him too. Blood. Before he could be counted on to clean up messy cuts and such. But now it was almost as if he didn't have the tolerance for any. Not even a little bitty drip.

"Dexter, wake up." He opened his eyes, wondering when he'd fallen asleep. Looking at the clock over the television, he saw that it was only one minute later. *"If you sleep now, they'll come for you. The Lord has told me that you're to be safe."*

"Safe from what?" Again his mind skittered. There was no other way that he could describe it. It was like a scratch on a record, and once it hit that area, it would just bounce or something. "What do I need to be safe from?"

"Everyone. You cannot allow women to touch you. I've told you this. You need to be pure. If you're not, then you will remain here after the coming of Christ and die with all the sinners." He thought of a woman, her face so beautiful that it made his heart burn with the need to touch her. *"Dexter, what did I tell you.?"*

Getting up, carrying his trash can with him, he entered the kitchen. Three days ago, when he'd been in here, there had been a box of donuts. Like a fool, he'd eaten them. His mother told him they were poison and had made him throw them up. Since then he'd not been able to eat any of the treats that someone, perhaps God, like Mom said, was leaving him. When he'd asked her why, with Dexter being the son of God, that he'd poison him, she didn't speak to him for over an hour. Sitting at the table, he found an envelope that was addressed to him.

He looked around to see if his mom was about. Dexter was amazed at her skills of coming up on him. Most of the time she'd just shout his name and he'd hear her. But seeing her, that wasn't happening. Not that he knew how she was doing it, but it scared him on so many levels that he was always careful as to what he was doing all the time.

The note inside was in his handwriting. And when he pulled it out to read it, he wasn't sure what he was seeing. The letters were there, but they kept moving around and around in a circle until he had to put it down and wait for it to stop.

"Dexter, you're in trouble." He looked around, wondering why he'd do this. "Run and find Tessie. Don't hurt her, but you find her and tell her that you need help."

That was all it said. No name at the bottom, and there wasn't any way for him to know the date either since it hadn't been postmarked, but was just sitting on the table. Getting up, he burned the letter in the sink and saw the ring on the little elephant's nose.

The woman came back into his mind. Her face was right there, and he could see her smiling at him. Her body was beautiful too as she made love to him. He heard her say that she loved him before the dream, or whatever it was, was taken away by his mom screaming at him again. Whoever this woman might have been, she had taken his purity from him, and he wasn't the least bit upset about that.

"What did I warn you about?" He wasn't sure which of the million and one things she'd been warning him about since he'd been a child that this might apply to. *"You're to stay away from nasty dreams. They're not going to get you into Heaven."*

Dexter was beginning to think he wasn't going to go anywhere near Heaven. Something—he'd done something that was going to prevent it. His mom didn't know whatever this was. If she did, he was pretty sure that she'd have killed him long before now. Or had him do something bad. Like the time she'd caught him with his cock hard.

He'd not meant for her to see him. Dexter had rushed to

the bathroom to see if he could make it go away. There had never been any talks of sex in their home. He didn't know how his body functioned that way. So when he'd had his first hard-on, the only thing he could think was to make the swelling go away. And touching it, that helped some.

Just as he was going to release—he knew the name of it now—just as he was ready to release, his mom had come into the bathroom with him. He had not been able to lock her out—there were no locks on any of the doors in their house except for the front and back door.

So just as he was releasing, she grabbed him by the back of his head and slammed it onto the wall. Stars had danced over his vision and he was aching then. Just when he was ready to demand that she tell him what he'd done wrong, she hit him again, this time in his painful cock.

After he was no longer hard, it took him several minutes of trying to talk to it before a cold shower was suggested. Well, suggest implied that she asked him kindly, when in fact, she'd turned the water on and shoved him in, clothing around his ankles and all, into the stall. He'd gotten a bad bump on his head then.

"You shave that off."

He wondered if his mom had meant his entire cock, but all she wanted him to do was shave all the hair. It had taken him longer than the other boys to get hair down there, them being so much older than him, and he wasn't keen on doing it. But she forced him to do so, plucking out the ones that he missed with the razor when he was done. It had taken him an entire year after that to be able to be in the same shower with any of the other boys.

Sitting at the table again, he thought about how much he remembered from his childhood. He and Tessie mostly, but there had been other children. All of them were imperfect according to his mom, and Tessie had been the only one that had defied her and continued to be around him. He'd gotten quite a few beatings from it, but he didn't care. Tessie was his best friend.

"Still is, but I need to keep her safe." Safe why, he wasn't sure, but he knew that it had to do with his mom. When he felt her coming toward him again, Dexter let all thoughts of Tessie hide away while Mom told him what to make her for dinner.

"*I don't know why you can't make me a decent meal, Dexter. I showed you everything that I did to cook for you.*" It was on the tip of his tongue to tell her he thought he was a better cook, and so was— Someone else was better too, but who? The name Alma came to his mind, but it, like a lot of his memories, went away almost before he could remember it. Alma was special. But he dared not mention this or her to his mom. She was angry enough all the time.

Dinner, like all the others that she wanted but didn't eat, was thrown in the trash. It took him a little longer to clean up after his cooking because he kept thinking of the name. Alma someone. He had no idea, but he would bet that his Tessie would know. Deciding to find her and ask what he could about this other woman, he didn't even tell his mom that he had plans for tomorrow. He'd just get up and leave before she woke. That way, maybe he could be gone and come back before she woke up.

Chapter 7

The clothing drive was going much better than he'd thought it would. Jules looked up as the next truck was backing up to where they had been putting the bags of clothing and the other things that were being separated into sections. There were even little bags of things like bottles of shampoo and deodorant and such that had never been used with the bags. He was so excited to get those too. Jules smiled at the next person who was helping him unload the bags of things from her trunk.

"I was thrilled to death to hear you were doing this. And on such a perfect day too. I don't think it'll be long before this lovely weather is full time around here. Oh, Jules, this is going to help so many people. Even when there is a fire or something, we'll have all this to help someone out instead of waiting for a sale or something." He told her that spring was only a few days away. "I know. And Jules, I wanted to tell you that you have mine and my husband's votes. The

Stantons have been good to all of us. You win and keep up the good work for this town, and we'll be viable again. I love that about your family."

"That's my plan. And I have a lot of them." He started naming off the jobs that Christian had listed that needed done immediately. "Also, as a family, we're working on a great many more things like this clothing drive. And next month we'll have a food drive, so you go ahead and start stockpiling those veggies. And for every one turkey donated, we'll donate another one as a match. I'm hoping to feed a lot of people this year for Thanksgiving, and then again for Christmas."

"Those are wonderful ideas, and I love them. But there are a few that you might not know about. Like the nursing home parking lot could use a good going over. Not just the trash that builds up now that it's closed down, but also the building could use some sprucing up." He asked why the home had closed and when. "Just last week, sadly. No funding. I thought when we voted that extra tax in, it'd be used for that. But no, it went to some other improvements. We sure do miss the center they had in there, Jules. There isn't anywhere else for us oldies but goodies to go."

"I'll look into that. And I'll get on that right away too. Christian has been helping us for the last few weeks, but he didn't mention the nursing home."

The next time he was working next to his mom, he asked her about it. "She said that it was lack of funding. Did you know about this?"

"I just heard myself. Mrs. Nash told me about it. She said that she just showed up to work one day and it was closed up tight. I had no idea. We have things planned for there. I'm going to have to find out where all those people have gone. There's Maggie Sue. I'll go talk to her. Her daddy was in there for a long time. And ask your dad too."

The rest of the afternoon was too busy for him to get many answers verbally, but he did find out from his dad what had happened. Apparently, it being not funded was only a cover story, for now at least. They'd had some drugs being run through the place, and the Feds had caught them at it. So much so that they'd closed up, arrested everyone involved, and chained up the doors. He'd have his work cut out for him if he wanted to get that going again.

I can help you with that. He asked Dane how. *Money. We have it. Not me personally, but we have the funds to not just get a newer building put in its place, but we can also do some improvements to the new place that would generate better workers. I'm in the process of getting it done now. I have connections.*

Will it be legal? When she laughed, he started to tell her no way. But she did tell him it was legal funding to get nursing homes a boost. *All right then. Can you look into it for me? I think we need this here just for Mom. She loved going over there.*

And those residents didn't need to be displaced either. A great many of them didn't have families around here close, and had to be shipped out. Terrible thing that. Two of them, I heard, couldn't be moved that far and were placed in another city, and passed away. It was just too much for them. He asked her where most of them had gone. *To local hospitals or other nursing homes too. And those were already overcrowded. And some of the things that the hospital does to them, the insurance companies won't cover, and it hurts the family. You need to get on this right away, Jules. This is serious money for the town. And you have company.*

He looked toward where she was and saw her nod, and following her glance he saw the mayor coming toward him. Jules didn't want to get into anything with him, so he turned toward the car that was just being emptied. Windbag pulled one of the bags out of the trunk and smiled at the person, thanking him for his help. Benny, from the wolf pack, just shook his head.

"I work here, you moron. See the yellow blazers we're all wearing? If you'd been here when everyone else was, you'd know that." Windbag's face turned bright red. Whether it was embarrassment or anger, Jules didn't know, but he did laugh at him when Benny continued. "You should just go on home. You're just like a blister, showing up when all the work is about done."

"I didn't know that this was on my calendar until I saw it on the news. I should have been informed so that I could make an appearance, Jules." Jules pointed out that he'd not told him about it. "A fundraiser, and I'm not made aware of this? That's not very sporting of you, Julian. What kind of game are you playing here? Or are you trying to make me look bad?"

"As you well know, I'm running against you. So, yeah, I'm trying to make you look bad. Actually, I really don't think I need to work hard at that, do you?" Windbag huffed and told him he didn't stand a chance, especially if he acted like this. "Acting like what? A man just helping out the community without fanfare? I didn't even know it was going to be on television. Not that I care. This is for the community, not for some kind of boost to my good name. I already have that."

He saw the woman from the local news station coming up

behind them. Jules decided to get some answers. When she pointed the camera at them both, he asked Windbag about the nursing home. Windbag looked right at the camera and put on his best face.

"I was just there this morning. I had a lovely breakfast meeting with the head of the department, and we're making great strides in keeping the people there happy and active. You should see the list of things that we have planned for this summer. Fundraisers like the one that we planned for today. Jules has been a big help to the community, and I, for one, appreciate it."

The news reporter did Jules's job for him when she started to point out that none of that was true. In fact, she was more polite than he might have been. Then he was sure of it.

"I'm sorry, did you say you were there just this morning having a meeting? That's not possible." He said that he was, even going on to say what he had to eat — pancakes and honey, his favorite. "I'm sorry, Mayor Windbreeze, the nursing home has been closed for over a week. That's what we came here to ask you about. I don't know who you had breakfast with or who made these plans, but that's just not possible since the last resident was moved out a week ago. Nor do I think any of the cooks have been there. Not for you or anyone."

The mayor was pissed, and even the reporter could see that. When the camera turned on to Jules, he smiled his best smile and told her that there was government funding they were looking into as a family. And once it was approved, a new building would be built with better facilities, as well as a person on staff that would help with keeping them active.

"And this clothing idea — while I'd like to take credit for

it, it was all my mom. She loves helping the community and is heartbroken that the nursing home has been closed. But I can tell you now, we're going to get something going for grants and donations to get something back up and running soon." Windbag tried again to take over the shot, but the newsperson wasn't having it. She asked Jules about running for mayor. "Yes, I'm running. However, I'm getting a very late start on it. I think, with the support of my family, my new wife, and daughter, I can make a pretty good showing in the standings."

"You keep up work like this, I think you'll do all right."

Her ear buzzed, and he could hear the anchor at the other end ask him about the other things that seemed to be happening around the town, like the veterans and handicapped gym. When she asked, he had an answer ready.

"My sister-in-law, Allie's father was injured a few years back on his job. And he can't use conventional machines in a gym. So, he came up with this idea that if he could find someone like him working in a gym, that he could maybe strengthen up his body a little more so that he can hold his new grandbaby when it gets here. Again, not my idea, but I wholly support it. Change and making things easier for people is what makes us all like to live here."

When his name was called, he excused himself. Jules was feeling great, but he also felt bad for Windbag. The man was standing in front of the camera now that he was gone, sweating like he'd been drenched in it, as well as stumbling over his words.

"You did well." He thanked his mom and dad when they hugged him. Dad continued as he looked over the mountain of clothing. "We have four women who are coming in tomorrow to help start sorting. We did get a start on that by asking that some of the bags be marked. And so you know, I had the boys go and get some items that were too big to bring in a car. Someone donated a washer and dryer. There are a couple of couches, as well as some beds. Now, I'm to understand that those things will have to be cleaned and steamed, but we can take care of that too."

"Yes, bed bugs. I'm not saying that anyone would donate those things with bugs, but we can't give them away without checking. This is fantastic, don't you think? And we got a really nice idea from Mrs. Bush. She said that we can keep things like that in storage for house fires or other tragedies." Mom told him she was proud of him. "You did this. Without your help we'd not have gotten even a quarter of all this."

"Twelve thousand pounds. That's what we're guessing. Most of it is clothing, but with the other donations, we'll have enough to help out some families when they need it." He looked over the other items that they'd not asked for. "We're going to need to clean up that warehouse on Fifth that we own. Just to store them."

"You could sell the building to the town, you'd get a tax break, and they'd have a place to store things. That way it's a win win for everyone." Dad said he'd do it. "I know you can, I'm just not sure how to go about it."

They were transporting the things to the warehouse temporarily when Windbag jerked him around. There were enough people around that they'd witness things if it got bad, so he was careful to hold onto his temper. He might have to later call the man out on this, but for now, he took whatever he had to hand out. Which just happened to be Windbag's fist, right to his face.

He didn't have to fall back, but he did, letting himself fall back hard on his ass, then the ground. And as soon as he hit his head, he wished that he'd taken better care that he hadn't. But almost as soon as he was down, his dad was hitting the mayor back. And it looked like he had used just enough of his cat to knock the man out cold.

"You all right, son?" He said that he thought so, but the blood on his hand when he touched the back of his head was caught on camera. *Play it up, son. This might be just the ticket for you to get yourself elected. Maybe even sooner.*

Almost as soon as Tess came to him, she handed him Ruby in the process. Jules did have a moment of regret for the older man. Jules hadn't wanted to make the man so mad that he'd resort to violence, but he hadn't done anything wrong. He'd not called the newspaper or the news. Jules hadn't hit him, nor would he. But his dad had no such trouble.

"I thought as a doctor, you'd not have it in you to take someone down." He laughed when Dad did. "You're my savior in this, Dad. Thank you very much."

"You're going to have a headache, I think." Tess winked at him. "I would like for you to come to the hospital and see about the bump. Better to be safe than sorry."

His dad spoke to him through their link when he was with Mom. *I'll talk to Christian about my hitting the mayor. That might not be such a problem since he hit you first. It sure is nice having an attorney in the family.* They were both laughing when he saw his brothers Wyatt and Levi talking to the news lady. He wished he'd gotten her name, other than just Lisa. *Looks like your brothers are talking you up. I heard Wyatt telling Lisa that you only started this campaign to get things going in this town. It's been idle for far too long.*

He thought about what had happened while waiting in the ambulance. The man had resorted to violence right away. Windbag had not just hit him, but had knocked him on his ass. A lesser man would have been hurt, like a human. What if a child had upset him? What would Windbag have done then? Taken his candy. Dad asked him if he was all right.

Dad, he hit me. Dad said that he'd been upset about being shown up. *I guess that was my intention, but I never meant for him to be fired from this. He will be, too. Someone will get a burr up their butt and he'll be asked to step down. The nursing home alone will be something that gets him into trouble. Not to lie to the public, that's one of the number one rules of being the mayor.*

He'll have to explain that one to the people here. Your mother will be the one doing that too. Asking him why he'd say such a thing, and why he'd not known about the nursing home. She does not condone any kind of violence, and when I had to hit him, and it was my pleasure, that made her twice as upset. You know her when she's upset. He did too. *Like I said, Jules, play it up for the camera. Not just for this, but because you hit your head and we don't want any questions on that either.*

The news reporters were in full force too. But he liked Lisa and the fact that she'd helped him out, though not knowingly, of course, but she had helped him. And her interviewing the mayor about the nursing home, that was a biggie too. He was bombarded with questions.

"Mr. Stanton, are you pressing charges?"

"What provoked him to lash out at you like that?"

"Are you truly going to take his place when he's asked to step down?"

The questions came at him fast. But instead of getting to tell them anything, Tess told them that she wasn't allowing him to answer questions; he might have a concussion and she didn't want him to say the wrong thing. He was in the ambulance before he could tell her that he was fine.

There were more news vans there when he arrived at the hospital. He wasn't sure what to make of it, so he just laid back and let himself be carried in. His eyes closed, he ignored the questions in favor of trying to think. Ruby was sleeping on his chest by then, making him feel a great deal better about life in general. Tess was barking orders that he needed to be let go inside, and when he was in a little private room, she kissed him on the mouth.

"You scared the shit out of me." Ruby lifted her head, then dropped right back down to sleep. Tess lowered her voice. "You do that again and I'll beat you."

"I didn't do anything." Tess kissed him again. "I love you too, but I wasn't doing anything to make him hit me. Well, I did, but at that moment I wasn't. He just hit me, can you believe it?"

"Yes, you're a good man, and I love you. And you did a number on him, showing the people around here what having a man like yourself in office can do for them. And don't be surprised if I keep you here overnight. You hit your head pretty hard, and I know you can shift it away, but for now, we're going to err on the side of caution."

"All right. Are you going to go before the cameras and let them know that you're keeping me? If so, I'd not mention

110

the fact that you're going to get lucky when you do. And that my mom is coming to get little Ruby so that I can jump your bones." She laughed and told him that he'd be lucky if he got lucky. "Oh, I will, love. I will."

~~~

Dexter moved between the buildings. He was sure that his mom was close, but he wanted to make sure that Tessie was all right. When he saw her granddad, he made his way carefully to where he was standing. The man smiled at him, but he looked tense.

"She's okay, isn't she? My mom didn't hurt her again, did she?" He told him it was her husband that was hurt. "Husband. She told me that, I think. And her little baby? She's all right too? Don't you think she is about the prettiest little thing?"

"Yes. She's my great granddaughter, so yes, I think she'd about the best little girl I've ever seen. But they're all fine. Are you all right, Dex? I've not seen you in a while." He felt his mom and turned to find her. "You're all right, son. I'm here if you need me."

"She wants me to kill the baby. No kids. No kids No kids." He snapped his mouth closed. "Please tell her that I'm sorry. That I don't want Mom to hurt her again."

"I'll tell her, but you should go and talk to her, Dex. She'd like that." He shook his head, and knew his mom was too close. "Dex, are you all right?"

"She's coming. Keep her safe."

His mom was right there then, like she'd been lurking and waiting for him to do something wrong. When she looked at Dr. O'Rourke, he did as well. "You're to keep that whore away from my son, Ericson. I've had this conversation with you before. Have I not?"

"You have, but they're adults now, and don't need you to keep them apart. Your son would have been better off had you been out of his life sooner." She asked him how he figured that. "You're a mean woman, and hateful to that boy."

"He's the son of God, and He gave him to me to care for. You're nothing. Not to anyone that means anything." When Dr. O'Rourke asked her what she meant, Mom glared before answering. "You know just what I mean. You're nothing because I say so."

"Your god, does he give you that power? To say when someone is something or not?" Just as he was sure his mom was going to answer, Dexter felt himself disappear. "Well, are you going to answer me?"

Debra hated that she had to share time in the world with her worthless son. He might be the son of her god, but he was stupid as shit. She wanted him gone from her life, but nothing would work in getting rid of him. Not even killing that baby.

The baby had been growing there, and God had told her that it had to go. That it would come between her power over the world and it. The thing was moving around like it was an infested worm, just eating away at the person carrying it. So Debra had done the best that she could, and drugged the woman up so that she could rid the world of the monster that she carried.

It had been easy to tie her to the bed, really. Debra thought that it had been that easy because the woman, Alma her name had been, knew that she was carrying a monster. Once she was tied down, however, and Debra made the first cut to rid her of it, she had screamed at her to stop. It was for show, she knew it.

It had taken her a long time to figure out where to cut. The monster seemed to know that it was being gotten rid of, and as soon as she made a cut over the womb, it would move to another part of the body. When she finally just sliced deep, killing it, that was when Dexter came back.

"What the hell have you done?" He tried to put the slice back together, but all he managed to do was spill blood on her nice clean floor. "Mom, you've killed him. You've killed your grandson."

"That thing is no grandson of mine. It's a monster. Just look at it. It's red, like the devil himself. God told me to kill it, to rid the world of his evilness. I cannot do anything but that. Now get out of my way so that I can finish the job." She hit the baby while Dexter was still trying to protect the thing, even after what she'd told him needed to be done. When the baby hit the floor, its body covered in goo and blood, she knew that she'd done the best thing possible and knelt down to pray.

But Dexter wasn't having it, and she had to hurt him too. Hitting him in the head, over and over, she decided that if he had to die too, then so be it. But he didn't, and when the mess of the woman — the package, she'd begun to call Alma — died too, Debra knew there was no hope for it, they had to bury it in the yard.

"You'll help me." Dexter didn't move from holding onto the dead monster. Debra thought for sure that he was going to bring it back to life, but it was dead, and she was thrilled. "Dexter, you need to help me get rid of this mess. Burn it all. That's the only way that the monster can be assured of dying."

113

He sat there for hours. No matter how many times she hit him, demanded or even begged him for help, he just sat there with the dead thing in his arms, rocking back and forth. Finally she gathered up the things that she needed, dumped the package on the bed, and then dragged it out of the house.

Burning it seemed to be too much trouble now that she didn't have help with it, so she dumped it in the hole that she'd used as an outhouse long ago. She knew that the hardest part was getting the monster from Dexter. Dexter was becoming too much work; even though he sent her money each month, she knew that he was spending the majority of it on his own whore. He should be thankful to her for what she'd sacrificed for him every day.

"Where is Dexter." She came back to the present and told the doctor that he was right where she wanted him. "And where is that? I don't see him."

"Of course you don't, dumbass. He's not here, but here. Inside of me." She wanted to shock him, but he only nodded. "You don't care that I have my son inside of me? The son of God?"

"I don't know what I think. Why do you believe you're holding onto him? Because right now, I see him, not you." That wasn't what she wanted to hear. "We found Alma and your grandchild."

When she lunged out at him, she fell forward. The fucking ass didn't even have the manners to keep her from hitting her head. Well, she'd fix him, and pulled out the gun to shoot him. All it did was click when she pulled the trigger. Dexter had lied to her. The mother of the son of God, and he'd lied to her.

Getting up, she reached for the doctor's throat. Dead, her mind kept telling her, kill him because he had brought children into the world. All doctors needed to be dead.

No kids. No kids. No kids. No kids. Her motto kept her sane while the world around her was going off the deep end. Telling him over and over while she strangled him, she smiled when his face began to turn a nice shade of purple. But she didn't want him to die just yet; she needed to explain to him why he was going to die. So letting off his neck just enough for her to feel him gasping for breath, she smiled at him.

"You are the instrument of evil. Bringing children into this world is what is going to make it come to the end, and only the chosen, the ones I deem worthy, will be there for my Lord to make sure that happens." He looked at her hard, and then he laughed. "You must die. There can be no kids. No kids. No kids. No kids."

The pain took her breath away. When she fell off the doctor, she tried her best to scramble back over him, to finish what she had started. But she was hit from behind again and again until she could no longer move. Falling to the side, she looked up at the man standing over her, and asked him why he'd do such a thing. But when it got closer, she saw who it was.

"You whore." Tessie, the whore, laughed. "You are going to hell. See if you don't. And when you are there, I shall piss on you and give you nothing."

"Pissing on me will be something you're giving to me. The pee, you see.... Never mind." Debra didn't understand, and she hated that the whore was making her feel stupid. Trying to move her hands to get them wrapped around the whore,

Debra saw the others there. "You're going to jail, whoever you are at the moment. And if I have to hire an exorcist to get you out of there, I'll fucking do it too. You have outstayed your welcome in our lives."

"I'll be back, see if I'm not. You whore." She told her that was getting old. "You are a whore, and you know it. When I'm back, I'll take care that you get your punishment. I am the mother of the son of God."

"Yeah, whatever." Then everything went black.

Chapter 8

Jules was as ready as he'd ever be for this. Some people, most of the town actually, had asked for a debate. Not on television, where he thought they'd have to go someplace, and he wasn't leaving his wife right now, but in the high school. He looked down at his clothing and wondered if his mom had been right about him wearing jeans.

"It'll make you seem like a person that doesn't mind getting his hands dirty. And you are willing to just step down off the stage and do whatever is put before you." She smiled at him. "I'm so proud of you both."

"You'll sit with Tess, right? I don't want her alone. It had to be the hardest thing she's ever done, just about killing that man." She said she was glad that she had done it; it had saved Ericson. "Yes, I'm glad as well. But she had to hit her best friend, and that has put her into a state of shock or something."

"I think she'll be fine, honey. She's just upset about what she heard too. And the fact that it was her granddad that was

117

being hurt by him. Or her, I'm not sure anymore." He told her that it had been Debra. "Oh, Jules, what are we to do now? He's trapped in that body, and he might not ever get out."

"We'll help him as best we can."

They would too. Even Wyatt was trying to find reasons that he shouldn't go to prison for this. All of it was going to get just one person in trouble, and that was Dexter. And he was as much a victim as the people that his mom had killed.

His name was called first, and he smiled at the people before looking at Windbag. He'd been practicing his real name since this thing was called. Windbreeze looked defeated, all right. But for whatever reason, Jules thought it was a scam.

"We have a few questions for Mayor Windbreeze first." The mayor brightened then, before going back to his beaten look. "You said that when the new taxes were put in place that we'd have enough to update and upgrade the school kitchens. But all we got out of it was a discounted microwave that others think you brought from your home."

Jules looked at his notes when Windbreeze started talking.

The microwave was used. I'm not sure it came from his home, but there were renovations done to his kitchen about a month after the money was approved for the school kitchen. He glanced up at Dane. *Those notes aren't going to do you as much good as I can. I know this man, probably better than he does himself. While he's not stealing per se, he is moving money around so that he benefits from it first. I'm still chasing money, so I don't have a handle on all that just yet. I'm missing something. Like the kitchen in his house. It was approved a month and a half after he had it done. I think with the money that was to go to the school. But right at the moment, I can't prove it. The renovations paperwork was all inflated too. The place was done with family help and for a fraction of the cost. But he got the money back, for overages and problems that they were supposed to have run into.*

Then how is that not stealing? She said he was paid back. *Paid twice, you mean. He paid for the renovations by using money earmarked for the school, then he was reimbursed for the same money when he turned in the bills, so he was paid twice.*

Dane laughed out loud, bringing the attention to her. When she waved for them to continue, she told him he was right and that she'd be right back. When she left, he wondered what she was doing when he figured out it was his turn to answer a question.

"Dr. Stanton." Windbag said that he wasn't the doctor, that his brothers were. He was just a retired cop. "No, you're wrong. Again. He's a Doctor of Law. And I think of law enforcement. All the Stanton men have doctorates."

"Why don't you ask me your question, Lessie?" She smiled at him. "I'm sure that no one here cares if I have a couple of degrees. I'm sure that Mr. Wind...Windbreeze knows as well."

No one spoke, but he did encourage the woman to ask her questions. "There are people that are looking for jobs outside our area. Just a year ago, the plant that was here to manufacture baskets turned away more employees. Can you tell me what you're planning for jobs?"

Instead of answering, he looked at his dad, who stood up to answer her question. "As a family, we've been working on some of the buildings in the downtown area. Of course we own a few of them, but right now, in addition to the workout place, we've set up a warehouse that is housing extras needed in the event of an emergency. Also, there are some foodstuffs that are headed to the pantry as well. My wife and her club have been having bake sales and the such every year to help give children the advantages that are needed in the way of book bags with supplies. Also, we have—"

Windbag cut his dad off. "The clothing drive was a great success, but Jim having a new shirt that someone else might have worn is not going to get us jobs. I think she asked you what sort of jobs you're going to bring to the community. And for the record, I have three in line now."

"Do you? Who?" He said that he wasn't at liberty to say at the moment. "Well, that's good that you're working on that. I have three major companies that are looking to bring us more work. Even a couple that are hoping that some of our people will help with the construction, as well as the setup of the new businesses. I have a line, a good one, on jobs that are going to need some people to help with road work. Not the actual work, mind you, but the everyday work such as flag holders. It's all good income for anyone that would like to help. As for the clothing drive, that was important. Not all of us have fifteen suits hanging in our closets, along with forty-four pairs of shoes." It was right on the money, and the mayor knew it. When Windbag stuttered about Jules sneaking into his house, Jules jumped on that. "You have that many suits and shoes? My goodness. Wherever do you wear those to? I don't see you out and about much, but you do seem to dress nice. I own a suit, but I'd much rather be in jeans any day. They're more comfortable in case I have to help someone out of a ditch or something."

Another dig to the man. Just yesterday the mayor had

120

driven by Mrs. Laddish when she'd had a flat. Jules didn't know if it was because of his suit or not, but he didn't care. He would have helped her, as most people would have. She was ninety-three years old and getting around good, but not good enough to change a tire.

"I have a lot of business meetings that I have to go to. And stopping to help an old lady that shouldn't be driving in the first place isn't part of my job." He seemed to realize what he'd said a moment or two too late. "I was running late, but I did send someone back for her. And called to make sure that she made it home all right too."

"Did you? I surely didn't hear you." He ignored Mrs. Laddish for the next question being asked of him. "You're an old poop, you know that? I think, like most of this here town, that we need someone that is going to get the job done. And even when you don't have to ask, them Stanton boys are right there to help you out. Why, just last month, one of them came by and plowed up my driveway. Didn't say a word. Wouldn't have even known but for the neighbor telling me who it was. Thank you kindly, Wyatt."

This went on for twenty more minutes. There were no more questions asked, but just people bashing the mayor for one thing or another. Then Dane showed up and had a group of suited men with her. She had never looked so serious about something since he'd known her.

After the meeting was called, he started toward her when he saw the small shake of her head. Dane was headed to Windbag, and as soon as she reached him, she told him he was under arrest and that he was being charged with a long list of things he'd done. The most important one was mail fraud.

"You falsified county records, then you sent the records to the courthouse via mail. And since Meggie down at your office keeps everything and anything that comes across her desk, I also know that you had filed your renovations a full three months after it was finished and paid for with the city school funds. She has the paid receipts as well. Then you used the money you got from the city for renovations, which you didn't pay for but stole the money for, to buy yourself a nice boat."

Windbag was yelling about misguided women and power going to their heads as he was taken out of the school. The county board approached Jules just as he was kissing his wife. Things had gone much better than he'd thought they would.

"Jules, can we have a word with you?" He nodded and said as soon as he said hello to his little girl. "Oh, it can wait. We want you to take over the mayoral term for the city. We need someone in there now, or the Federal Bureau will assign us someone from their office."

"I can't step on their toes, Mr. Blanchard. They're the government." He explained why he needed him to take it now. "Oh. You think this is going to stick, these supposed charges against Windbag?"

"I do, and I love the name you've given him." Jules felt his face heat up when he realized what he'd done. He told him he was sorry. "Don't be. He is a windbag. But as to what we need from you. We'd like you to take the office for several reasons. The most important one is the fact that we all know and trust you. The second is your knowledge of the law and how it pertains to what is going on here. We don't want to be called on anything that will get the city in trouble. And I believe it will. We've been made aware of a few things by your sister-in-law that need to be looked into as well."

"As much as I'd like to help you out, Mr. Blanchard, I should talk it over with my family. My wife has only just found out that we're having a baby, and we were hoping to have time to get everything set up before I might get to take office." The room had been set up before Ruby had been born, but these guys didn't need to know that. "Can you give me some time? Say until tomorrow? I have to talk with all my family."

"Yes, yes, of course. But don't be surprised if we have a word or two with your father. He can be a very persuasive man when he needs to be." They all laughed. "All right, tomorrow then. We'll meet in the office. The Federal men, they're cleaning it out as we speak."

He acted stupid in that moment, not wanting to give away how Dane knew about the house because of him. "What is going on, if you don't mind me asking? I mean, am I going to be getting a mess if I take this position?"

"Yes. I'll be honest with you, yes you will. While I can't tell you everything, the school board is most upset with the way things have shaken out. Also, Dane — a very nice woman, by the way — she's been helping with finding where our money has gone. The taxpayers' money has gone. Did you know that it's been put into offshore accounts? Not all of it, but a big part of it. And there are some shady dealings going on with the crew that is supposed to be doing the work too. His own brother has been the lowest bidder on all the contracts, and we've not even realized it. Going under his wife's maiden name. I'm ashamed that we didn't catch that before." Dane joined them and asked to speak to Mr. Blanchard. "Well, duty calls. I do hope we can count on you tomorrow, Julian. I surely do."

Jules was almost home when he was contacted by Dane. "Apparently, there was more than a little bit of missing money. There were also quite a few checks made out to a woman by the name of Estela Rosa. If it's who I think it is, then he's going to prison. Estela is a madam that deals in women that are discreet. I'll talk to her in a bit. Damn, Jules, you're getting a mess." He said that he'd not taken it yet. "You'd better. I've been doing this work just for you, buster. If you don't take it, I'm going to sic your mom on you. That'll change your mind quick enough."

"It is a mess, Dane, a lot more than I think I might be able to handle. I mean, just to the end of the term is only four months. What can I do with that to prove that I'm worthy of the job?" She told him. "Okay, not the best answer, but I do like that you think I can do one thing at a time and get it taken care of. All right. I do have to talk to Tess, then to Mom and Dad."

"Your dad is already having business cards printed. I'm not sure, but I think your mom is looking over office patterns for your new digs, and Tess has her own set of issues. You'll take it." He laughed. "All right. I have to get going. You have a nice evening."

Jules thought he would. When he got home, Ruby was fussing, teething he was told, and Tess was crying, hormones. He wouldn't have it any other way, he thought, than this right here. Having his own family was better than he'd thought he'd ever enjoy it.

~~~

Colton wasn't sure that he was going to be able to talk to Dexter. Wherever she had him, he was deep within the elderly woman, and she wasn't budging so that he could talk to him. Colton started to rise when he thought of something that his dad had said earlier, something about Dexter being alive, and did the mom know it.

"You had a lovely funeral." The look on her face was priceless, and he sat back in the chair. "The entire town turned out. I thought, and I think it was the opinion of my family, that they only turned out to make sure you were dead. You've not been the nicest of people."

"I don't need to be nice. And I haven't any idea what you mean about a funeral. I'm right here, aren't I?" The voice was different, he noticed. Harder than she'd been talking to him before. "You just keep those thoughts to yourself and answer my questions. I want to know why I'm in here. I want to bring charges up against that whore, too."

"Tess is no more a whore than you are." He pretended to consider that. "Well, that might not be right. She's married and having another baby. But you've never been, have you? How many children did you have before you kept Dexter?"

The shift from woman to man was quick. And had he not been looking at Dexter, he might not have noticed. But before he could speak to Dexter, Debra was back.

"I'm not a whore. I've only had the one child, and he's the son of God." He asked her what god she was referring to. "Why, the Almighty one, you moron. What the fuck is wrong with you?"

"Does the Almighty allow you to speak like that? I would think he'd want you to be humble and forgiving. You don't sound very forgiving when you speak of killing Tess." She called her a whore again. "You don't like her, do you?"

"You think not? What a fucking moron. Yes, I said fuck again, and I'll say it again and again. Fuck, fuck, fuck —"

"You've had four children, not including Dexter. And all of them by different fathers. And there isn't any record of you losing them, so I can only assume that they're out there. Correct?" She didn't even look at him. "I've found all but two of them. Want to guess who they are?"

"No, I do not. I don't care one bit who they might be, if there were any other children. My Lord picked me to have his son, and you'll not sully that with your lies." He said that he wasn't lying. "Of course you are. I don't have any other children."

"They were taken from you. The state where you lived, they found you to be unfit and you were stripped of them. I think that word is very appropriate, don't you? Since you were a prostitute at the time of your arrest, and the two children you had then were taken from you. Margo and Mike, their names were." He saw him again; Dexter was fighting with her to come forward. "Why don't you let me talk to your son? Dexter, are you there?"

"You have no right to try and turn him against me. He's the one that got me into this mess anyway, and I think that he is just fine where he is. Did you know that he helped me kill that baby? Yes, he did."

That was all it took for Dexter to fight his way to the

forefront. As soon as he was free, screaming as if being born again, he looked at Colton with frightened and exhausted eyes. Colton didn't know how much time he had, so he spoke fast.

"Your mother is dead. Someone poisoned her to make it look like a heart attack. We've found Alma and your son; they're being laid to rest in the family cemetery. Tessie is taking care of the arrangements. We've found two other bodies there. Do you know who they might be?" He shook his head and started twitching. "Dexter, fight her. This is your body — fight her so that you can get rid of her."

"She wants to kill Tessie. And her daughter. Protect them." He said that he would. "Alma was all that I had in the world." He screamed again, this time sounding like he was in a great deal of pain. "I never killed them. My son died in my arms when she cut him from my fiancée, for no other reason than she could. You have to protect Tessie. She was always good to me."

"You can beat her, Dexter. Tell your mother to go fuck herself and come back to us."

He cried out again. His nose was bleeding when he finally dropped to the table. Colton wasn't sure who was going to be speaking to him, but he hoped it was Dexter. Through it all, he only had Tess on his mind.

"What did you hope to win from this? Your show of force." Debra. "He's weaker now. Easy prey for me to take over. What do you think they'll do to him if he's free to come out? They'll kill him. And if they don't, I will. He's a sap. A fool, I told him over and over again, no kids. And what does he do? He has one of the monsters."

"Monsters? Is that what you think his son was? Your grandchild?" She screamed, sounding of so much hate that Colton leaned away from her. "You killed your own grandchild, and if you keep this up, you'll kill your son too. Is that what you want? To kill him? What do you think your god will do if you succeed?"

"There is no God." He felt the chill of her words down his back. She looked quite mad then, her lies simply gone. Her words were harsh, a little slurred. "There was never a god talking to me. Christ, he's hurting me. Tell him to stop. The story was to make him behave himself. To make Dexter never make me a grandmother. Not that he'd have been any good at being a parent, but I would have been happy never to hear those words uttered to me. I didn't want him to reproduce. No kids. No kids. How many times must I say that until I get what I want?"

"You're dead." She shook her head and waved at the borrowed body. "That's not yours. That's Dexter's. And when he takes it back, what do you think is going to happen to you? You'll be as dead as your grandchild, as dead as Alma."

The laughter made his skin crawl, like something foreign and evil crawled over him. When he opened his mouth again, not even sure what he was going to say, she slammed her hands down on the table and made him jump. Colton stood up and felt the entire weight of the room, the evilness of the woman/man before him, take him to the floor.

When he woke, his mother was leaning over him on the gurney. Fat tears were rolling down her cheeks, and he knew that he'd scared her. He'd been afraid too and sat up and grabbed her. Holding her tightly, like he had when he'd had bad dreams as a child, he sobbed out how much he loved her, how much he would never treat her badly again.

"Colton, you've never treated me badly. But I want the hug. You frightened me." He told her how afraid he'd been as well, that she'd ever believe it. "She's dead."

"What?" He looked at her face, not understanding at all. "Who's dead? Debra? She can't be, Mom—if she is, then so is Dexter."

"He is as well. Dexter left you a note. He hung himself not five minutes after he was taken back to his cell. I think it was too much for him." He nodded, taking the envelope from her. "I've never been so depressed in my life as to know that that poor boy suffered so much. She did this to him. Killed him as surely as she'd hung him herself."

He laid back down, feeling as drained as he'd ever been in his life. The envelope would have to wait; reading it here, in this hospital, would feel like a betrayal. He wasn't sure why he thought that, but the hospital hadn't helped him, and he wasn't going to spill his story here where anyone could come in and listen.

According to the paperwork that he'd found on the young Dexter, he'd been hospitalized nearly monthly when he'd been between the ages of four months to seventeen years. He knew from Tess that he'd graduated from high school early, then college had been easy as well. From then on, he'd led a normal, if not backward, life.

He'd had broken legs; his arm had been broken more times than was humanly possible. Yet the hospital had never reported any of it, never called the police, nor had child services ever come to the house to check up on the supposed accident-prone child.

Then at the age of thirty-five, after spending his entire adult life without his mother's influence, he made his way home again and introduced her to his pregnant fiancée. Things from that point on he knew little about, but he'd been speculating for days now.

Debra hadn't given in to her nature to tell him what a fool he'd been. Otherwise, Colton thought, he would never have left his fiancée with her. The baby would have been fawned over, there might have even been a gift or two. They had found wrapping paper at the house. Then on the last day, Debra had taken her chance and killed both the fiancée and the child.

They weren't married, he knew that. But it mattered little to him. They were mates, as surely as if they'd been shifters. And when they created their love in the form of a child, they'd become man and wife to him.

After being released, he was glad to see that Jules and Tess had come to get him. They took him home, and Tess never said a word. He did wonder if she blamed him for it, and asked Jules and he told him no, she was upset that Debra had won in the end. Taking his letter to his office, he sat down at his desk and opened it. Inside was an insurance policy made out to him, for ten million dollars. The letter was dated two weeks ago.

Chapter 9

"Dear Colton, I know that I should be writing to my friend, but this is the only way that my mother will allow me to write. I do hope that you know who it is I'm speaking about. Tell her that I loved her, my whole life. She's been my little sister since I first met her. And my biggest protector too.

"The insurance policy is for you to use for something to do with mental health. I don't have any idea what that might be, but please name it for my wife and son. His name would have been James Shipley. Please don't name it for me. I have...I am a man that wished only to be happy, and that never happened. My family, Alma and our son, they were all I had, and I wasn't able to protect them as I should have. I lost them because of myself.

"I'm going to end things when I get the chance. I don't know when that will be, but I know that you wished to help me with my issues. All of the Stantons did, and you've no idea how that made me feel. But I've had to do this, so that she cannot take control and hurt others. I'm sure you understand. I don't know where she ends anymore and I begin. I think it's been that way my entire life."

Tess looked at Colton when she got to this part. He'd read the letter, he told her, and thought that she should as well. She asked him about the money and the fact that he committed suicide. Surely they'd not pay out for that.

"There will be cash from the policy. He made sure that when he was seen in the room with me he wasn't himself. That alone will go for state of mind, I'm hoping. If not, then I'll match the money myself and do as he asked." Tess thanked him. "No need to, Tess. He was a good man."

Picking up where she'd left off, she continued. "My mother killed my father. I don't know who he might have been. As you know, my name isn't Jorden, or if you don't know, then I cannot help you. He was dead long before I knew to ask for him. And that only happened the one time. She was not happy when someone questioned her, as you might have found out.

"You will find his body in the back of the property where there is an old stone fence. I would go out there every time I would think of him and add another stone there. As you'll be able to tell, I went to see him a great deal." Colton told her that there were thousands of stones, and that Mr. George had been exhumed and put into the cemetery.

Nodding, she went back to reading. "I should like to tell you something that you should pass on for me. "When I was seventeen my mother destroyed all hope of me ever becoming a father or to have sex like a normal human being. I need not tell you how that happened, but I was injured in such a way

132

that I couldn't father any children. I suppose that was her way of making sure that I never made her a grandmother.

"That, I've come to understand, was her greatest fear, and the reason that she made up talking to the Lord. I think, after so long, she might have believed her own lies. Whatever happened to her, she manifested them onto me and made me less than a man, less of a person.

"The child, my son, you're asking yourself; who's was it? I don't know. Neither did Alma. One night when she was coming home from her job, someone jumped her, and she was raped by several men. The thought of losing the child to some kind of drug never entered her mind and I took her to my heart, and I would have the child as well. Much like Jules has done for me and the child of my sister.

"She meant the world to me, that one. When things were getting bad at home, which was often, I would go into my head and think of her. The things that she'd have said, the way she would have taken me away. She did in a way; every time I thought of her, I would run away from where I was and be happy. Even if it was only for a moment.

"There is money in my account. I've called the bank were Alma and I banked and had all the money put in the name of Ruby Stanton. She, of all children in this world, deserves a head start on life, a chance of happiness and friendship like no other. I understand that there is money for her from her father, but this will be for something special. Especially for her. I wish for her to enjoy life in a way that my son never got to do."

Tess was crying now; the hurt of this man, the bigness of his heart for her daughter, was overwhelming. While she continued with the letter, she saw the young boy that she'd grown up with, the child turned man. And the profound suffering of them both.

"There are other things that I'd like for you to take care of for me. I don't know how this will come about, but I'd wish for you to bury me next to my Alma and child. They were mine as much as I had anyone in my life." She paused to gather her heart to her chest, where it beat hard for this man and his life. "My mom...I know not what to tell you about her. She had been insane all my life, and I should have tried harder to run from her. But it got to be too much, so I just left when I was old enough. Help others, please, so that they will be safer than I was.

"Alma was killed that day. I don't remember much about it other than to say that I was there when my son died. He was in my arms as my mom took Alma away, taking his last breath, so to speak, when he never had a chance. I have wished with all my heart now that I had never left my home that week, never given in when I should have remained strong for them. I will never forgive myself for leaving my wife and child to her. We'd be alive and happy had I never trusted the façade that she put on for me. Now Alma is gone, my son James is, as well as myself. My mother, she did this to us.

"I wish to tell you to hug my friend for me, every day. Tell her that I will never forget her. Nor her granddad. He, too, was important in my life, and maybe, had I been able to stay with him, I'd have had a different life. But alas, I did not.

"I thank you for what you've done for me, Colton. Thank you for everything." Then it was signed Dexter Shipley. Forever yours."

Tess cried for the next half hour. Not all the time, but when she remembered Dexter and how he had thought of her, even to the end, her heart would break again. Going to the office where she knew that Jules was working, she sat down while he finished the phone call he was on.

After he read the letter, she sat on his lap. They didn't speak, but just held one another. Jules was her life, and her daughter's too. From this day forward, she decided she was going to live each day like it was her last, and be happy even if she had to— No, never that, but she was going to take charge of her life and be the best at what she could be.

"Change me." He looked at her face. "Right now. I want you to change me into a cat. I want you to make me a cat so that I can run with you and be like you."

"All right." He picked up the phone. "I have to make arrangements for Ruby. You and I will be down for a few hours, and you'll be out for days. She will be upset, I think, seeing you like that."

After his mom and dad came to get the baby, hugging her and telling her that they were sorry about Dexter, she waited in the living room for him to come to her. As soon as he entered the room with her, she asked him what he wanted her to do.

"You need to be naked." Nodding, she began taking off her clothes. "Do you know what is going to take place? Have you talked to Dane or Allie?"

"Yes. They said that it's painful for a little while, then I'd just black out. That when I woke, I'd have to turn the volume down; that I didn't understand, but they told me I would. Are you really going to do this?" He nodded and pulled his shirt

135

off. "You have to be naked too?"

"I do. I'm going to make love to you first, then when we're finished, I'm going to be my cat, and then we're going to change you. You understand that my cat must do it." She nodded and smiled at him. "You're entirely too calm about this. I thought you'd be nervous."

"Oh I am. But I want this too much to be scared of it. I don't want to be—? Will the baby be all right?"

"Yes. I asked Mom about that a couple of days ago, and she said that it would be fine. Stronger for this, and so would you be. You'll feel the child differently as well. More in touch with it. I don't know the sex right now, but you more than likely will be able to tell." She told him that Dane told her it was a boy. "Well, she would know. I'd like to name him after your friend, if you don't mind."

Tess started to cry again, and he held her. "I'd like that as well. Dexter was my friend and a monster, his mom, treated him like he was nothing more than a thing. The things she did to him." He held her while she sobbed again. "James Dexter Stanton, if you don't mind."

"Perfect."

He helped her undress, and when she was naked, he dropped to his knees in front of her and pulled her pussy to his mouth. As soon as he pulled her clit into his mouth and bit down gently, Tess came apart. This was going to be epic.

He made love to her with his mouth and hands. She was fondled, her body warmed by his hands. When he moved his mouth to her thigh and then to her knee, she moaned at the feeling of his thicker tongue, and looked to see that he was still a man but different somehow.

"Lie down, love. I want to explore you." She did as he asked, holding onto him as he helped her to lie down on the floor. And when he leaned over her, tasting her body everyplace he could, she tried hard not to come. For some reason, she wanted it to be huge, and this was her way of giving him something too.

"You're making it hard." He sat up and fisted his cock, making the precum drip on her belly. "That isn't what I meant, but I want you."

"You have always had me, Tess. Forever." She felt her heart fill with her love for this man. "When you come, I'm going to shift then bite you. Are you ready for that?"

"Yes. Make me your cat, Jules. Please?"

She watched him settle over her, his cock right at her entrance. And when he punched forward, not just her body came apart with the climax, but her mind as well.

Colors danced behind her eyelids. Her hands felt like they could pull magic from the room. And when he came too, bringing her over the edge again, she held onto him, afraid that she would fly away with the passion of his love.

The first bite wasn't that bad. But then he was only tasting her, he told her. Jules grinned at her as he let his cat take him. And when he licked her breast, the feel of his tongue made her come again. Just as she was peaking, the massive teeth of the cat entered her shoulder.

~~~

Jules didn't want to hurt her, but he knew that he had to. This was going to make it better for her, make her stronger for them both. But almost as soon as his cat bit down on her thigh, he knew things were going wrong. Her blood tasted weak, and he knew he was going to lose her.

Brayden, come to me now. She's dying. He told him that he'd only just begun. *No, you don't understand. Something isn't right. Come here. Bring Dane.*

They arrived just as her heart was slowing to almost nothing. Dane shifted, her sleek cat larger than even his. But when she bit down on Tess's other leg, he could tell that she knew it as well. That Tess wasn't going to survive this.

Brayden let his cat take him. When he told him to bite her where he could but not in the belly for the child's sake, Jules did as he was told. This was to save her life, and he'd do anything, anything at all, to not lose the only person that he'd ever loved.

It took them another hour to get her stable, but they still weren't sure about either the baby or her. When Brayden told him they'd have to finish the job or lose her, he bit hard into her belly and into the womb. They would lose the child for sure, but as they were young yet, he told him, they could have others.

Picking her up from the floor when her heart finally started to beat better, he took her to their room and Dane helped him dress her in his shirt. She was so pale, deathly white. Jules wouldn't leave her, not even to take a shower. But Dane bullied him into it, and he stood under the water and sobbed like he'd not done since he'd been a child.

The phone in the house was ringing when he returned to the bedroom. He didn't want to talk to anyone right now, and was grateful that Brayden seemed to have a handle on it. When he touched her hand, he knew that she still wasn't going to make it, and promised her the world if she'd just wake and look at him.

"We did everything we could." Jules told Dane that he knew that. "She had cancer. On her brain. Not anything we might have noticed right away, but that's what you were tasting when you bit her. I can feel that it's shrinking, the tumor, but as far as it being gone, I just don't know what will happen now."

"I didn't know either. I mean, as soon as I bit her in the shoulder, I knew that she wasn't going to make it. She was too weak, I guess." Dane said nothing, but he could feel her sorrow. "If you don't mind, I'd like for you and Brayden to go on back home. I'm sure you have more to do than to sit here with me."

The pop to the back of his head was so much like his mom that he turned to look for her. "What the fuck is wrong with you? She's my sister, and I'm not leaving her here. You're my brother, you moron. I'm not leaving you either. What the fuck? You wouldn't leave me if the roles were reversed, and I'm not leaving you. What a thing to say to me."

"I'm sorry." He did grin then. "I thought you were Mom. I swear, you hit like she does. I'd hate to think this, but I almost feel sorry for your children."

Children. He knew that the baby Tess carried now would soon abort on its own. There was too much trauma to her body for it to be able to survive it. Nothing had happened so far, but it was only a matter of time. When Dane stood up, cutting her wrist with her ever present knives, he watched as a few drops of her blood fell along Tess's lips.

"It can't hurt. And my blood has some extra shit in it that might help her." When she did that every ten minutes, he could feel Tess's heart slowing again. "I'm so sorry, Jules."

It took another twenty minutes for her heart to stop beating altogether. Wyatt had been called in, as well as Colton. Both of them worked on her for two hours, trying their best to get her to be all right. But all it did was prolong the inevitable. Tess was gone from his life, and he had killed her.

"Mom, she's—"

Mom stood over her still warm body and slapped her. It was the cruelest thing he'd ever seen his mother do. Just as he was standing up to—well, he didn't know what he was going to do when suddenly Tess not only sat up, but gasped for breath as well. No one moved as she sat there.

"What happened?" Tess looked at him, and then around the room. They were all there, and he would imagine that not one of them looked happy to see her. "Did I die or something?"

"Yes." She nodded at him, then shook her head. "You died. Just seconds ago. Then Mom hit you and you came back to me."

"You hit me?" Mom sobbed and hugged her to her. "I love you as well, Lucy, but hitting a woman when she's down, that seems sort of harsh. But I do thank you for it."

They were laughing then, all of them, as they each hugged her to them as if she'd been gone on a long trip and had only just returned. He sat on the side of the bed with her when the rest of them went to make something to eat for her. She said several times that she was starving.

Jules crawled into the bed with her. He wasn't going to leave her right now, perhaps not ever. But holding her, feeling her warm skin under his hand, he was glad that Mom had hit her, but didn't understand why.

"I had a dream when I was...well, I don't know where I was, but I had this dream. I spoke to Alma." He didn't tell her that she more than likely had. But since he wasn't sure what happened to a person when they died and came back, he said nothing. "She told me some things. Things about Debra that someone should know."

"Right now, I don't care. Unless it's important." Tess told him it was, but it could also wait. "Dane and Allie went to talk to the family yesterday. They're taking it pretty well, I guess. They said that they had already figured that she was gone, but it's good to know that she's home. They didn't tell them about the baby. Dane said that it was just too hard on them knowing that their child had been murdered."

"I think that's for the best. Did they know about Dexter?" He said that they had met him once and had liked him a great deal. And he'd been there when she'd been hurt. Again, they didn't seem to know about the rape, only that she'd been robbed at gunpoint and hurt." Tess nodded. "You think they should have known about the baby?"

"I would have wanted to know. I'm assuming that I lost ours." She didn't say anything when he told her that he was sure too but didn't know when it would happen. About then, Wyatt came in to give her an exam.

Jules was glad that his family was being so helpful. But he also wanted them to leave them alone. To just let him be with her. She had died, he was sure of it, and his mom had saved her life. He would need to ask her why she had hit her, what made her think that would work. Reaching out to her while Wyatt did his thing, she laughed.

I was angry, to be honest. But I read once that sometimes a

141

shock to the system could jumpstart a heart. Or in this case, her mind. I think she would have been very disappointed in herself if she hadn't woken up. He said that he might have been as well. *I didn't have any paddles, nor a machine like your father has in the basement of our home, but I thought, it couldn't hurt. She's doing well then? The baby is still intact?*

What a strange way, he thought, to ask if she'd lost their child, but he told her that Wyatt was seeing to her and he'd let her know when he was finished. When he came into the hall a few minutes later, Wyatt was smiling.

"You're a very lucky man." He said that he knew that too. "The baby seems to be fine. I've checked, and his heart rate is much better, as well as he moved. I would like to take her to the hospital to make sure with an ultrasound, but I don't foresee any problems. But I would like for her not to shift for at least a week, Jules. And bed rest for at least that long. When you bring her in next week, I want you to carry her to the car, bring her in with a wheelchair, and make sure that she eats well."

"I will. I promise. Did you say this to her?" He said that he did, but he wanted them both to know. "And sex is out of the question too."

"Yes, for now. I'd also like to look at her head. Dane said that the tumor was gone, but I'd like to see if it being gone has caused her any trouble. Or if it's just smaller and not gone. All right?" He told him he would do whatever it took. "I'll tell the family about the baby. But I'm also going to caution them about over extending their visits. She needs quiet and her daughter. She asked me about her several times when I was in there with her."

He didn't go in right away after Wyatt left him. Jules was too emotional to even go and get Ruby to bring to her mom. So, as he made his way down the hallway toward the nursery, he was glad now that his mom had brought her home to be with Tess earlier this morning.

She was napping when he got into her room. The nursery had been moved around since they'd brought her here. The bed was against the wall where she could see out the window. The trees, he thought, would bring her a lot of joy. They had even gotten her a birdhouse to hang on the window, so she'd be able to watch a bird if she wanted. Tess said that she was going to put a flower box outside her window as well, to bring her butterflies.

The pink had been toned down a little by painting the walls white. The carpet was pink, as was the ceiling fan and everything else. It wasn't so difficult to enter the room without your eyes hurting. When his daughter woke up and looked at him, Jules smiled and spoke to her.

"Hello, my darling. How did you sleep?" Picking her up when she reached for him, he took her to the changing table to put a fresh diaper on her. Also, he put her in one of her pretty little outfits, one that made her look especially adorable for Mommy. The entire time he was cleaning her up, he talked to her about her new brother, the way they were going to have to get a bigger car, as well as having to learn to play ball together.

"I suppose we have time for the latter of those things, but you never know."

Jules was laughing when he entered the bedroom to see that Tess had fallen asleep. He found himself wanting to check on her, to make sure she was breathing, then she opened her eyes and smiled. Ruby went right to her mom and snuggled under her breast.

"There's Mom's little girl." Ruby sat up and looked at her. Her first teeth were just starting to come through, and she was being a trooper about it. "What have you been up to? Mommy has turned into a big kitty; what do you think of that?"

Ruby jabbered her answer and they both laughed. Molly, their new cook, brought in a tray that was filled with all kinds of delights, and then one for Ruby. It surprised him when a high chair was put in the room as well.

"You should know, sir, that the baby monitor is on in her room. We have one that lets us hear when she's awake." He tried to remember what he'd said to the baby, but Molly patted him on the cheek. "You're a good daddy to your little girl. That's wonderful that you can change her, and fuss about buttons like we all do."

"They're very tiny, aren't they? I thought for sure that I was going to need to get some tape to make it stay closed. Staples were my first choice, but I was afraid that they'd stick her." They all laughed. "Thank you, Molly. And if it's not too much trouble, do you think we can have our meals up here until Tess is better?"

"No problem at all. Dr. Wyatt came by the kitchen, stole a pastry or two that was marked for the miss here, and said that she wasn't to get up. We've located a table and chair that we can bring up today. This little thing was in the kitchen for Miss Ruby, and we won't need it while she's here with her momma. If you need me to take her, you just holler. She's the best thing this house has ever had, I'm thinking."

Jules had to agree and was glad that she was as happy with the staff as she was with him. Playing with Ruby was fun — mind numbing at times, since she didn't have conversations just yet — but she was a great deal of fun, and he loved her with all his heart. Her mom too.

Chapter 10

Jules hated this part of working. In fact, he'd rather be home with his wife, but something needed to be done about this man, and he was in the mood to do it. When his dad showed up, just getting in his car, he asked him what he was doing.

"You're here to make sure that the little Rogers boy is all right. I'm here to make sure that the Rogers dad makes it out of the house all right too. Besides, your mom sent me, and you know how she can get." He asked his dad if Mom knew he was afraid of her. "Oh yes, I'm sure that she does. You guys are as well, I'm thinking. Otherwise, you'd not be sitting here waiting to go into the house to make sure that a little boy who could very well be falling out of a tree isn't being hurt by his father."

"What if I told you that I don't think it's the father?" Dad asked him why he'd think that. "I don't know. I've been doing some research, and I don't think it's him."

"The mother?" Jules shook his head. "Then that only leaves the children, and I'm sure that six-month-old Becky isn't doing it."

"The grandmother moved in about two months ago. She's supposed to be bedridden. And that makes me wonder why no one has questioned him being hurt all the time. I know, also, that there have been some loud arguments between the parents. I think they're blaming each other.... But it's almost time for the mailman to come by, so we'll wait." He didn't have to wait long before he saw the mail person coming up the walk. "She's there all day with the baby; who, by the way, has been crying a good deal more than she did before all this. They think it's teething. I think it's Grandma."

"Why do you suppose the mail lady can help you?" Jules said nothing while the mail was put in the box at the house. Then just as plain as day, the little old woman came out of the house a little, snatched the mail, and a few minutes later, put it all back. "Well I'll be danged gone."

"I think she's the one that's been taking her checks. The office told me that they've all been in there several times over the last months, her complaining that the mail service is stealing her checks. I got to thinking about that, how they don't turn up and why not. It had to either be Peggy, the mail carrier, or Mrs. Rogers, the grandmother."

A few minutes more went by before little Scott got off the bus and then moved to the side of the house. This might have been curious if he'd not seen the boy do this before. He emptied all his paperwork, or what appeared to be paperwork, from his backpack, then hid whatever it was under a stone. Going to the house, the kid looked like he was going to the gallows instead of into the loving arms of his grandma.

"What do you suppose that was about?" Jules said he didn't know. That yesterday when he'd been looking for it, it was gone by the time the house was settled for the night. "Could be bad grades. I'm not saying that this is the way to go, but it could be that he's hiding them from his family and that gets him into trouble."

"I don't know. I've spoken to his teacher. She said that he's really good at turning things in and getting his work done on time. She said that while she knows not to have a favorite, little Scotty is." Dad told him that made no sense. "I know that too."

The scream of a child had him getting out of the car. As they were crossing the street, he told his dad to follow his lead. Then he made him put his bag down. It would do neither of them any good to come running like they knew someone was going to be hurt.

When Jules knocked briskly on the door, it took Scotty a long time to answer. When he did, he looked up at Jules with a blackening eye and a bloody lip, and Jules had his dad take him to the car while he dealt with the woman. As soon as he closed the door behind him, he heard her shouting at Scotty.

"Get your skinny ass back in here. I'm not done talking to you right now. I asked you where your homework is." When she came around the corner, he stood as still as he could while trying to remember if he'd turned his body cam on. "What's the meaning of this? How did you get in here?"

"I thought you were bedridden. That's what Tom told me anyway." She fell to the floor, screaming for Scotty again. Kneeling to her level, he could see that she was thinking, and thinking hard, on how to get out of this. "That won't work now — I've seen you up and about."

"Scotty did this to me. He's forever tormenting me and dragging my poor old body off my bed. Put an old woman back there, won't you, Julian? I will be ever so grateful."

He wasn't surprised that she knew his name. What he was surprised by was that she would go to such links to try and pull the wool over his eyes.

"Where is Scotty?" She said that she ran him off. "Ran him off? Why would you do something like that? What is he, seven, eight years old?"

"He hurt me. I told you that." She moaned when he picked her up, and he saw the big bag of food near her table. "Scotty again. I have to keep the snacks in here that his mother buys for him, or he'd eat them all."

"Scotty certainly seems like a bad little boy. How did he get the bloody lip?" She didn't say anything, but since he was holding her, he knew that she stiffened. "Nothing to say, huh? What is it you tell his parents when they ask? A lie, no doubt."

"I'm calling the police." He put her on the bed with a bounce. "I'm going to tell your mother what sort of person you are. What do you think that pretty wife of yours would think?"

"That you're a monster. I've been dealing with people like you a lot lately. And I have to say, you're about the worst." He turned when he heard his name and looked at his dad.

"I have to take him in." He nodded. And that was when Mrs. Rogers decided that she was in deep shit. "He's got a black eye, and I think a concussion. I'm calling the police too."

"He's forever falling down. Tell them, Scotty. Tell them

that you're forever falling down and that I have to clean you up." He said nothing, and Jules thought that was very telling too. "Scotty, so help me, if you don't fix this, I'm going to tell your mother on you."

"She doesn't like me." Jules told him that his mother loved him. "Not mom; she does love me. But that that old biddy, she don't love me at all."

"You're a liar. He's lying to you." Scotty went into the other room with his dad, or so Jules thought as he turned back to Mrs. Rogers. As soon as he turned his back on them, his dad yelled but it was too late.

Scotty pulled out the gun from Jules's back and shot four times point blank at his grandma. She was dead before she fell back, and Jules took the gun from him. Scotty had been pointing it at his own head when Jules took it, and that bothered him on so many levels. The baby Becky was brought from the hall closet by his dad, and she'd been hurt too.

The police arrived a few minutes later. Scotty wasn't talking by then, and the little girl had been examined by his dad. Six months old and she had two broken ribs, as well as one of her fingers had been broken.

As soon as his parents got there, Scotty started crying. "You killed your grandmother? Oh, Scotty what are we going to do now?" Jules asked to speak to them and took them in the other room. "He didn't mean it. I know that he's a good boy, but lately he's been lashing out. I don't know what to do with him anymore. But he'd never kill his grandma."

"But he did. I was there. And I have it on camera." Mrs. Rogers, Rebecca, started sobbing. "I was here when she had just hit Scotty. And he had a bloodied lip as well as the black eye. He told me that she didn't like him at all."

"They've had their moments. But I think it's because he has to watch her for the half hour between the time he gets home from school and we get home from work." Jules told him it was more than that and had them sit down. "You're not going to show us him shooting her, are you? Jules, that isn't right. Please."

"No, I want you to see what we saw when we got here. My dad joined me." He nodded, pulling out his tablet. "This part is when I came in the house. You can see that Scotty is hurt even then. My dad, he took him outside. He'll explain that in a moment."

Jules watched their faces. He knew the exact moment when they saw her as he had, walking around like she wasn't injured. Tom looked up at him, then back at the video to finish watching. He turned it off just as he put her on the bed.

"She can walk." He nodded. "No, you don't understand. We have been paying someone to come here every day and work with her."

"I've been out front since you left for work this morning. No one shows up, nor does anyone come by to make her dinner. She did leave once, to get into a car and then come back with a bag of snack food. That's been marked for evidence. Gloria told me that Scotty eats it when he comes home, and that you put it in her room so that he'd not have access to it." He waited until what he was saying sank in. "Also, you should know that she picks her checks out of the mail and somehow destroys them I don't know how, but I'm sure that she was either putting them out with the trash or burning them. The house smelled of burnt paper when I came in."

152

"This explains a lot of things." Jules nodded. "Scotty, he killed her, he really did. I know that, I believe you, but he's only seven years old."

"I think this time he was protecting Becky. You told me that she'd never been hurt until the last couple of days. And that you thought he was doing it. I think Scotty killed Gloria because he was afraid that you'd never believe it was her. My dad will talk to you now."

Dad came in and sat at the kitchen table and passed them a stack of papers. "They're his papers for school. He does them on the bus, leaves them outside or in the shed, and gets them as soon as he comes out to get on the bus in the morning. He does the same thing with all his graded papers. As you can see, he's been getting excellent grades this entire last few weeks. Before that, you can see, the correct answers have been erased and then the wrong ones put on his paper. I think that his grandma was doing that to prove that he was a bad kid."

"Why?" Jules nor his dad had an answer for Rebecca. "She had no reason to harm either of our children. We brought her here because we thought that she was hurting for money. This explains why we had to pay the physical therapist in cash, doesn't it?"

"I just don't know what to say or even think." Tom looked up when he saw the medics taking his mom out of the bedroom. There would be trouble, Jules knew, but he thought that Scotty would be fine. It was his parents that he worried about. Tom spoke again. "I thought all along the neighborhood children were picking on him, and that he was lashing out at my mom because he was scared. We even took him to classes on self-defense, the ones that Christian's wife does."

"Yes. And I don't want you to be alarmed, but—"

"You have to take him in. I understand, but I don't have to like it." When they didn't move, he waited for them. Dad didn't say anything either as Rebecca continued. "He came to me a couple months ago and said that Grandma hated him. I thought it was just that he was jealous of Becky, and that she was getting to spend more time with their grandma. I never dreamed that.... You said you found her in the closet. That she was wet and dirty?"

"Yes, I took care of her diaper and put something on her bottom. But she has some broken bones. Her finger and a couple ribs. Someone is going to have to own up to hurting the little girl, but I think it's clear who did it." He wondered how long the child would have had to sit in her diaper before it got changed. Or did Scotty have to do it when he got home? Either way, it was starting to add up for the family.

~~~

Tess was looking over the paperwork for the staff meeting when Lucy came by. She'd been popping in and out of the hospital for the last few days. And she almost always brought her a little gift or something from her husband. Her office was beginning to look wonderful, thanks mostly to her.

"I've just been down to the nursery." They both looked over at the crib that had been brought in for her daughter when she was there. "There are ten new babies there. And two of them have no parents."

"What do you mean, no parents?" She explained how they had been dropped off, a no questions asked sort of thing. "You mean they've been given up. We used to have that

154

happen several times a day where I worked before. It's sad, but I'm so glad that there is a way for parents or sometimes a single mom to get help like this."

"Usually the children are adopted right away, but these two, twins, I don't think they're going to be so easy." She asked her why. "They're cougars. The parent isn't from our pack, but they did come into the hospital smelling of perfume so that we'd not be able to find them. I wonder if they know how this program works."

Tess wanted to go and see the twins. She'd had the strangest dream last night about twins, and needed to make sure that it had only been a dream. Tess asked Lucy if she'd keep an eye on Ruby while she was gone.

She was nearly to the nursery when she heard her name. Allie was coming with her, and they seemed to have the same determined look on their faces. Tess paused long enough to ask her what she was doing, and she said that she'd had a doctor's appointment and wanted to see the nursery. Tess told her what she was doing.

"A dream, huh? You thinking of adopting them?" She said no, then yes, then no again. "Well, I certainly understand that. What do you think Jules will say about that?"

"Thanks? You did good? I don't know. But I'm only going to see them. For now, anyway."

She saw them the moment she stood in front of the glass. They were beautiful. Pecking on the glass, she asked to come in and showed her badge. Allie was allowed in as well.

Tess fell in love with them both. From the tops of their heads covered in red hair to the bottoms of their chunky feet. They were adorable. Asking the nurse what she knew about them had her laughing.

"They're a pair, that's for sure. When one of them cries, mostly the heavier one, the other will put her hand on her face and she calms down. When feeding them, you don't have to feed them both at the same time, but you do have to hold them together, just so they can touch skin to skin. I'm not saying that they were ever neglected, but I will say that the mother would have had a hard way of it, handling them both at the same time." She asked if they were all right. "Oh yes, Dr. Stanton. Perfectly fine little girls. And they're good too. Not even crying much when they're wet or hungry."

"Tess, what are you doing?" She smiled at Allie. "Are you going to adopt them? If you are, I'm going to be very jealous. I love little red headed girls, and they have so much hair too."

"I think that I am. I want them to come home with me now." She reached out to Jules and he said he was never too busy for her when she asked him. *There are two of the cutest little girls here at the nursery.*

I'm sure they're not even close to being as cute as little Ruby is. Nor my son when he's born. She told him he would be handsome, not pretty, but that wasn't what she was saying. *Then I don't understand.*

We need to adopt them. He was quiet for so long that she filled in the space. *I know that'll mean we have four children under the age of one when this one is born, but we can do it. I'll even go down to part time — that's what I was told I could do when I took this job. Also, we have the money, and they're going to need us because they're cougars too. Like we are. They need us —*

Slow down, baby. These twins, have you kidnapped them? I mean, you said they were in the nursery; the person you're planning to take them from, do they know this? Tess told him not to be silly. *Silly or not, I'm sure that someone will miss them. Especially when you said they were cute as a button.*

They're drop off children. As soon as the parent or parents drop them off at a shelter or hospital that takes them, they forfeit all rights to the child. Or in this case, our children. He laughed. *They need me, Jules. And I need them. I don't know why, but I really do want them to come home with me.*

Let me finish up here and I'll come there. You might be wrong in how beautiful they are, and I just want to make sure. And if there is some kind of paperwork that we'd have to fill out, you get a start on it. Tess told him that she loved him. *You might not think that if the nanny quits or you see the first semi of diapers coming to the house. We'll be in the poor house, too, if you plan on adopting each child that comes to you like this.*

I'm not making any kind of promises. You'll just have to love me more. He said that he did, every single day. *I'm going to have them ready when you get here. I'm sure that the staff will be sad to let them go. They're that adorable.*

I'll be there as soon as my meeting is over. I have several meetings tomorrow too, so if you find one tomorrow that you think we should adopt, then you'll have to make that decision on your own. She was laughing when she told Allie what was going on.

Getting the paperwork ready was much easier than she thought it would be. Both of them were certified to adopt a child—her because she had been bonded when she got the job, and Jules because of the paperwork he'd completed when he started carrying a gun. Not to mention, the nursing staff had started the adoption paperwork as soon as she showed up to look at the children.

"You'll have to name them." She looked at Allie when the nurse told her that. "I'd say that you should talk to your sisters-in-law about their names. You don't want to pick something that they have."

Allie told her both girl names that her and Dane had decided on. "And you're having a boy, so that helps. So, what do you think? Lucy's middle name is Allison, and I don't think I ever heard what your mom's name was. For that matter, if your parents are still around."

"Both died when I was younger. I don't remember them at all." Allie said that she was sorry. "Thanks. But my grandma's name was Asher, believe it or not, and her middle name was Leanna. So, how about Leanna Asher and Julia Allison, or something like that. I'll let Jules decide."

She couldn't wait to take them home with her. Pushing the little bassinet down to her office, she showed them to Lucy. While she was looking them both over, holding them and fussing over how pretty they were, Jules joined them, and fell in love just as she had.

And he thought the names were absolutely perfect, just as she was. She wondered if he was going to really buy diapers wholesale like he had threatened her. Formula might be a better thing to buy in bulk.

Chapter 11

Levi loved having someone helping in his studio. And Ken was such a good guy that he was enjoying talking to him as well. When he was finished with a painting, or something else that he was working on, he could just walk away and know that his brushes would be cleaned up, as well as his area. He was even getting more work done.

"Levi, you should know something. That picture that you had me take pictures of and printed up? Well, the ladies at the photo shop really liked it." He giggled; the man actually giggled. "I think they want to hang him up like a pin up girl or something."

"They called here asking me where the man was. I didn't tell them that it was me. Can you imagine what would happen if they found out?" Ken said they'd corner him in an alley. "No. I was thinking more along the lines of— You're hanging out with Dane too much. You're beginning to sound just like her."

He laughed this time, and so did Levi. Painting that picture had been fun. But when he'd added the background and the other elements that he wanted, the painting had taken on a life of its own. And the woman in the painting, who no one saw but him, scared him a little. Not like a nightmarish kind of scared, but just gave him a little jolt to the belly.

They worked for the rest of the morning, and when Ken left to go to the shelter for lunch, just to hang out with his wife, Levi went to his own home. The staff was off for the day, and he was trying very hard not to mess up his house. He really did hate messes, but he despised cleaning up. Laughing, he pulled out the sandwiches that had been left for him this morning.

In two weeks he was going to be in Germany for a showing. But he was actually leaving on Monday. In four days. And he was going to be gone for a month. Long enough for him to take a walking trip around the country, take some pictures, and relax before starting all over again when he got home.

He was depressed.

Levi had never been one to suffer depression much. Just an occasional bad morning or something that his painting or art could blow away. But just lately he'd not been sleeping well, getting up in the middle of the night to paint, and his appetite had gone downhill. He looked at the three sandwiches on the plate, wondering why he'd only eaten half of one of them.

"You need to get laid." He smiled at Colton when he came in the house. "What's up? I can feel you're not happy all the way to the office."

"I don't know. And don't psychoanalyze me either. I'm just a little down." He sat a box of chocolates in front of him.

160

"You want me to be your valentine? I think we're a little old for stuff like this, not to mention, we're brothers."

"No, I got it on sale. Half price. It's the fifteenth. I'm assuming you forgot. Again." He said that he had a standing order at the florist to send all the women on his list flowers, and Mom a plant. "How romantic. And what did you give the lady in your life?"

"I don't have one." Colton ate two of the three sandwiches left as Levi opened the candy. "Do you suppose with all the others getting mates, we will too?"

"Nope." He asked him why not. "Have you met the women in our family? There cannot be more like them out there for us. Wyatt has said he's not going to see women anymore in his practice. And you never leave the house or studio, so that's a no-go. And me? I don't care if I meet her. One way or another. I mean, I would love a mate, but I just don't see it happening in my line of work. Anyone I see is going to be off her noodle, so no thanks."

"What a horrible thing to say." He just shrugged. "I'm not sure about finding her. I suppose that she's out there someplace. I'm worried too, that, she'll be like…. What's her name? Brayden's first almost wife."

"Vonda Hull. Yeah, that is sort of scary. So was she." He agreed with his brother. "I've been thinking about things though. I mean, like you, I have a house. No staff, but then most of the house is empty anyway. I've lived there five years, and all I've managed to do is buy me a big bed. I have a dining room table that I scavenged from the barn one day. Two chairs that I use because I'm too busy to mess with bringing the others into the house. I use paper plates too."

"What are you going to do about it? I'm assuming that you've come to some sort of awareness." He nodded as he ate three pieces of candy. "Well? What are you going to do?"

"You and me, we're going to go shopping. But not at the traditional kind of stores. I want something that reflects my taste." Levi asked him what his soon to be wife might think. "She'll love it, right? If she's my mate, then she and I will have the same tastes. Old as shit and covered in peeling paint."

"You're weird." Colton grinned at him. "All right. So, we're going on this road trip sort of thing. When are we leaving? You do know that I have a show coming up?"

"I do know, and I also know that you have all the paintings and pottery already sent over. That you're ahead of the game, too, for it and the next one, which is local. You can afford to take the next ten days off with me and go on this trip. We need it." He was right, Levi was well ahead of himself. "And Wyatt is going too. We're going to have a single man bash and go shopping. Ten glorious days of just the three of us, manly shopping."

"And how do you propose we get these things home? I'm assuming you have this all worked out." Colton got up and poured them both a glass of milk. And got out a box of cereal. "What the fuck are you doing?"

"I'm starving. Like you, I've not been eating well. And so you know, while we've been talking, you've eaten candy, another sandwich, as well as two apples. You're hungry too." He looked around at the counter. "I made you two sandwiches and you ate them both."

"You're doing that psycho shit on me, aren't you?" Colton told him that he didn't have to. They were just talking. "Okay,

162

so I might need this break. But I can't just up and leave. I have staff, a house. I even have employees."

"I've talked to the staff, and you're packed to go. They even packed you some clothing that doesn't have paint on them. Ken is going to get paid while you're away because he's going to be working at the shelter with his wife. He's happy for it. Your mail is being picked up with mine and Wyatt's, and the way we're getting our things back here is by truck. I've hired a driver friend of mine who could use some work, and he's going to come with us, but behind us by a couple of days. It's all arranged."

Wyatt showed up a little while later, after Levi had three more sandwiches and drank two glasses of milk and a glass of water. Not only was he suddenly starving, but he was dry as a bone too. His brother was right, he needed this.

They were packing up the truck to go when he asked Colton about his bags. He pulled out his credit card and said that was it. "I don't have any casual clothes. Not a single pair of blue jeans. I own several T-shirts that look like I've had them, and I more than likely have, for the last ten years. All of them have either football, college, or logos for something to do with town. I have a pair of tennis shoes that I hate. I'm going to find things I want to wear and wear them. As I go. Even my underwear is old. Christ, I should have done this years ago."

"How the hell did you both get the time off? I mean, I know that you work for yourself, but it had to be hard." Wyatt told him how they were supposed to be going to this doctor's convention. "And you decided this would be better?"

"No. Yes. What I mean is, the convention was canceled

about a month ago. We decided then that you were going to go with us. It wasn't until we talked to Ken and found out that you'd taken care to be ready for your next show that we decided not to tell you until we were leaving. Everyone, little brother, knew but you." Levi didn't even care. Colton grinned as he continued. "You are going to let loose, right? I mean, no calling home to make sure that your paints are all capped, and that whatever you do with that clay, it's all secure too."

"No. No more than you will." Colton laughed, and they loaded up. "What do the others say about this? I mean, you have told them, haven't you?"

"I have, and Brayden is jealous. Christian is planning a honeymoon with his wife before the baby comes. And Jules and his wife are overrun by children. They're really cute having those kids with them. Can you believe it? They look like they're all their kids. I mean, I have no doubt that they'll be treated the same, but damn — four babies at one time. I love being an uncle, don't you guys?"

"I think of it as practice for us all. And if we never meet our mates, then we'll be the best damned uncles around." Levi wondered if Wyatt felt that way, but didn't ask. This wasn't going to be a time of arguing. It was going to be fun. "I'm joking, Levi. I want to meet her."

"I know that. So do I, but not right away." They looked at Colton, who was next in line. "You think it works that way — oldest to youngest?"

"Yes, I hope so." He looked at Wyatt, who was younger than him by nineteen months, as Wyatt continued. "Yes, I surely hope so. I don't have a house. No staff, not that I need one in my apartment, and I have some growing up to do. I've seen the way the women in this family can make you toe the line, in a good way, and I'm not sure I'd be any good at that."

They were on the road twice. The first time they left Levi's house, he had forgotten to lock up. He never locked his doors because he wasn't ever gone from his place. But when he decided that he might have forgotten to turn off the stove, Wyatt reminded him that he had had cereal. A grown-up food.

"Hey, I love it. I can eat it standing up. If I forget to wash out the bowl, it's not that bad. The milk can be nasty, but I do have Ken now, who comes and cleans up for me." He laughed. "I'm thinking he needs a raise. I have never had anyone but Mom fuss at me the way he does, and is nice when I'm finally doing whatever it was he wanted. Like putting the sponges that I don't want in the trash and not throwing them at him."

"You still do that? I remember once you said you were going to soak them in paint and make a painting that way. Did you ever do it?" He pulled out his phone and showed his brothers his art. "You sold that too, didn't you? For a great deal of money. Some nasty sponges soaked in paint stuck to a canvas, and you sold it."

"I certainly did." He didn't tell him that it had been fun, or that for days he just went at it, throwing the sponges at it to relieve some stress. Then one day, someone came to his studio to talk about a painting he wanted for his home and bought it. Levi did that now all the time, relieved stress with his art. It was fun and profitable.

He was actually thinking of setting up another one for Ken to work on. The man was stressed out. Waiting for his wife to go into heat, that would do it, he supposed. And if it sold, he'd give him the money too. For his kid's college fund. Yes, his life was beginning to take on a new journey.

~~~

Jules loved the little girls in his life. He loved everything about his new life, actually. When Julia was finished having her bottle, he put her over his shoulder and patted her back. This one was going to be trouble, he knew it from the start. Laughing when she belched like his father did, he laid her on the couch beside her sister and picked up Leanna.

"What to do with all these females in my house. I know, buy a big lock so that no one touches you." Tess laughed with him as she fed Ruby. "How did we get so lucky? I have all these women in my life, and I could not be any happier than I am right at this moment."

"Remember this when they're all teenagers at the same time, and this little guy I'm carrying is upset because his sisters are taking up all the bathroom time. I think we should consider that now. Put them each in a bathroom of their own." He didn't think that would work and told her. "I know. Those two there, they'll be together for every little thing. I've never seen babies seem to need each other like they do. Do you suppose they're all right?"

"Yes." When Julia started to fuss at him, he put her on his lap so that she could touch her sister while she had her bottle. "If you'll notice, I was able to feed Julia without having to hold Leanna. I think we're making progress."

The twins were newborns, not much older than about a month, if that. They were a lot smaller than Ruby, and with the fact that they were twins, they were still tiny to him. It had taken him an entire day to get up the nerve to hold one of them, he'd been so afraid of hurting them with his big hands. He looked up when his dad joined them, taking Julia off his lap and holding her.

"A man could get used to this. Holding a grandchild is the best thing I've ever had the pleasure of doing." They had decided not to dress them in matching outfits, and Dad had told them he thought that was smart. But his mom didn't agree, apparently, because everything she bought for the girls there were three of everything. "I have a question for you. The girls' room—you going to just put two more beds in there, or are you going to have four nurseries when your son comes too?"

"I don't know what we decided." He looked at Tess, who was burping Ruby. She had gone to bottle feeding now because of the new baby coming along. "Tess? Did we?"

"I just thought for now they could all be in the same bed. But Ruby is rolling around now, and I worried about that. But the twins, they need each other, so I'm not sure that they'd like to be separated." Dad told them that they'd have to be sooner rather than later. "That's probably true. I'm worried about that, if you want the truth."

"I know the family." That was surprising, and he asked his dad how he'd found out. "I'm a doctor, son. I know who has children in this town, who is in heat, or ovulating if you will, and who is having twins. This little girl, the one that had these little girls, she came to see me one time. Not as a doctor, but to ask me about adoption. It took me some remembering but your mom pulled some records, and while I know she didn't give me her correct name, it was easy for Dane to find her."

"What do you know? I mean, the kids, are they all right? I know physically they are, but anything.... I'm freaking out here, Dad." Dad said that they were fine. "But you talked to her, didn't you? You went to see her?"

"I did. How did you get so smart?" He told him he was a cop. "You are. Always and forever, I think. Yes, I went to see her. She's only a kid. Sixteen and living on her own. Lisa was raped by the new alpha, and when he found out that she'd conceived, he assumed she was his mate. But she's only half cougar; her mom is human, so it doesn't always work that way. Anyway, he raped her one night and she conceived, like I said."

"They're girls. He didn't want them?" Dad shook his head slowly. "Where is she? Dad, tell me so that I can make sure she's safe."

"She is now. Living in Europe, staying with some friends of ours. She's not going to come for the girls. Lisa knows that the girls are in good hands, and that you won't turn them out because of who they are and what they are." Tess asked why that would matter. "They're alpha children. Girls, yes, but they might be alphas someday should it need be. The fact that they're so close is because she had to hide them all the time when they were first born. Not just from the alpha, but her family as well. They were shamed, you see, that she'd not given him sons. Messed up badly if you asked me. But she came here, looking for a place that takes children without anyone asking questions. She knew what she was about. By her giving them up, without a birth certificate or names, no one would associate them with her."

"They're not from here. I mean, not even this state." Dad

told him they were born in Ireland but wouldn't be able to claim citizenship there because of there being no certificate of birth. "That is so sad. I mean, to come all the way here to give them away. It must have been the hardest thing she's ever done. Besides giving birth."

"She'd done that on her own too. Birthing twins without nary a bit of help." His respect for the mother went up off the spectrum. "I showed her pictures of the nursery. And of them with their sister. You can imagine that she's very happy."

"Dad, what are you not telling me? I can't take anything sad anymore. Please tell me that she's all right. I beg you to even if you have to lie." He said that she was just fine. "Then what is it? Tell me."

"Nothing, son. I promise you. I'm thinking that you need to get out more. You're becoming as bad as your momma, waiting for the other shoe to drop. Oh, did I tell you her roses came in yesterday? She's so excited that she wanted to go out and start digging up the yard. I told her we'd have to wait at least a few more days. You have to make sure that they're going to be readied to this area before putting them in the dirt." He explained to Tess about Mom's garden and Vonda, who had destroyed it. "She was something else, that woman. And nutty as a fruitcake too."

"Sounds like it. I was wondering about something. You said that the others were on a shopping trip and would be gone for a week." Dad nodded, and Jules remembered that he'd asked them to find him a couple of things for his office. "I was wondering what they're doing this for. I mean, isn't there a place that can just go and get it for them? Like an antique shop that's not someplace they have to go to?"

"They needed this. Every year since they were doctors, Wyatt and Colton go to the convention. This year it was cancelled for some reason. I wasn't going—I haven't in a long while—but they decided that they were going to take Levi with them. He's been in a funk." Tess asked if they knew why. "Yes, I'm thinking he's ready to hang up his paintbrushes for some reason. He's into a lot of other media, but painting has been his favorite. Anyway, I see him going to teach. I think he'd love that."

"Teach? You mean at the local school?" Jules told Tess that it would more than likely be at the college level. "Why not teach down at the shelter? I'm sure that there are people there that would love it. And it's good therapy too. Painting stimulates the mind for some."

"I'm going down there today and do some crafts with some of them. Not as a teacher, but as a learner. They're going to have a couple of classes on how to do stained glass. I might not like it, but I'd surely like to try. And next week they're going to have a glassblower come in. You hiring that girl, Sandra, has been perfect. She has been bringing in someone each week for the past month." Jules mentioned how Ken was working with her while they were gone. "Yes, and you know what he does? Made me laugh. He tans hides. Not the kind like him, but beaver and others. I guess there is a real market for it. But I never would have guessed that as being a hobby for a wolf."

Lunch was ready and Dad decided to stay, but Mom was coming as well. She came in the door and reached for the babies, not even caring which one she got. It just happened to be Ruby, and she was delighted to see her grandma. Mom said pretty much the same thing his dad had said about holding a baby. Nothing like it.

Ruby was sitting in her chair and having part of Mom's lunch when she just looked at him and said "Da-Da," again. He was stunned, much like he'd been the first time. Of course, she wouldn't say it again, but she did clap every time he said it to her. Jules thought that was the most beautiful sound he'd ever heard, to be called Da-Da, and he asked Dad how he'd felt the first time it had happened.

"Well, Brayden, as you know, wasn't keen on talking much when he was little. He'd point and then point back at himself with his hands. Then when he did open up to speak, there was no shutting him up." Mom said that you still couldn't. "Yes, that's about right. Then when Christian came along, I swear to you, it was almost as if he were a lawyer already. He would sit and study things before making any kind of decision about what he wanted and how much of it. The rest of you, including you, took to talking like you had plenty to say and you weren't going to waste any time in saying it."

The girls were laid down for their naps and Jules needed to get to work. Unless needed, he'd only work after lunch on Monday, Wednesday, and Friday, and then on Tuesdays he had meetings and on Thursdays he'd do paperwork. So far it had been working out well, and he was getting more done than his predecessor had ever done.

Walking to his office, he waved at some of the people and stopped to talk to a couple more. Things in this little town weren't great, but they were getting there. Jules stopped to watch the construction going on at the school. A new cafeteria, as well as new playground equipment, was going to be nice.

"Hello, Jules." He nodded at Mr. Hamby. "I was wondering what you're planning to do with the old wood that you take out of the building on Sanders Street."

"What wood? Oh, you mean the old flooring. Nothing that I can think of, but then my dad owns that building. They're in pretty rough shape. Did you want to build yourself something with them?"

He shook his head and started to explain. "I've been off work for some time now. I have a lot of woodworking equipment that was my dad's and father-in-law's. I was going to try my hand at some goo-gaas like they sell at the arts and crafts show in the fall. I get unemployment, but I was thinking that I'd try and make some extra money for the kids' band and stuff." He asked him where the show was. "Not far from here. I was hoping that sometime this summer or so, we could get one started here. But the mayor, he was never for it."

They talked all the way to his office. And by the time he'd left him, Howard Hamby was going to see what it took to get an art fair started. They might not have many come this year, but Howie said that he thought it would be a good time to start, what with the town starting to perk up a bit.

When he got to his office, a group of people was waiting in the lobby. He hadn't any idea what was going on, but he went on up to his office. Mrs. Crock, his new secretary, was there waiting for him. He asked her what was going on.

"They want to have a street party." He nodded. Jules wondered if Howie had told someone already. "The band, they took second in state, and you know that the football team did just as well. They want to celebrate in the street, and try and raise some cash while they're at it. You know, selling things they might have made. We used to do it a lot more when the baskets were in full swing."

"Call Howard Hamby, tell him he's in charge. I think he'll do it."

They were both laughing when she left him. Picking up the phone, he called his mom.

"Mom, what do you know about street fairs?"

Chapter 12

Colton watched the people look at the items in the sale. He didn't care for tag sales, but auctions he could get into. He'd done a lot of them in his younger days, when he would flip things for cash. Today he was in the market for some things for his own home. Wyatt came up to him just as his turn came up to get a bidder number.

"Can I bid on your number?" He told Wyatt that was fine. "Good. Can he have two cards? That way we can keep them separate."

As they were walking away, Colton asked Wyatt what he'd been looking at. "Believe it or not, not too much. I just love coming to these things. Where is Levi?" He said that he was flirting with the woman at the pop stand. "Figures. Anyway, you have your eyes on anything?"

"Yes, several things. There are a few desks that I really like." He took him to them, but neither of them really looked. They didn't want to show anyone they were interested in them. "I need a house, though."

"Yeah, I just heard from Dad. Did you know that the old mayor's house is for sale?" Wyatt said he loved that house. "Well, good, he bought it for you. And before you ask me how much it was, I haven't any idea. All he told me was he got a good deal, and that he'll see you when we get back. If you want the desk, he said that the house is empty but for a few things. He's having the refrigerator and stove replaced today. Dad said they were nasty."

"Great." He agreed with him. "All right then, time to do some serious looking. Oh, you should have a look at the stuff back in the house. Man, that sucker is nice. It'll go for a bit, solid oak, but it's really nice."

Wandering around, Colton found several boxes that he'd like to bid on and wrote those down. There was a table and chairs that would have to be cleaned, but he liked them. Once in the house, however, he changed his mind about the table out there and fell in love with the one in the house. Now this was a table for his family.

It was oak, like the rest of the furniture in the oversized room. It was an Amish table, where everything had two uses. This could be a table or a deacon's bench. The entire top of it lifted up and was the back of the bench. The solid wood top had been made from two very different woods, which he thought was done on purpose.

He was just sitting it back on its base when a little old woman came to join him. He'd not realized that he was the only one in the house.

"There are chairs that go with it, one at each end, and large backed benches that go down both sides of it. My husband's grandfather made this." He told her it was lovely. "I do so hate to get rid of it, but there just isn't any room in my condo that they're moving me to."

"I'm sorry to hear that." Forever the doctor, he wanted to cheer her up. "Being way out here in the back of this farm, I bet you aren't as social as you used to be."

"No, not anymore. I've outlived three husbands and a cat. Liked the cat more than I did the husbands." He laughed. "I have a lot of family, and most of those I don't care much for either. All brats, even my own kids."

"My mom has six sons, and we still listen when she says to jump. Just before I left, she told me to call her when I get to each place on our trip." She asked if he was here with his wife. "No, two of my brothers. I'm not married."

"Grandma?" She woo-hooed at the young man. "They're about to begin. Mr. Ploughman wants to know if you've decided on this table or not. Do you want to sell it?"

"This young man just made me an offer I can't refuse. He's getting the chairs as well." The young man congratulated him, and when he left them, Colton sat down on the bench of the table and patted the seat. "I suppose you'd like to know what that was about."

"I do. And the deal that you and I made. I do want the table, but you had something else in mind, I think." She said she did. "Your name is Mrs. Spencer, correct?"

"Alma." He felt his heart race. "I had it in my head to sell it, then not to sell it. But when I saw you looking it over, being so careful with the wood, I knew you'd have the perfect place for it."

"I do. How much do you want for it?" She told him that

she'd get to that. "I knew of a woman once, named Alma, but she passed away before I could meet her. She and a very good friend died at the hands of another."

"That's so sad; why would you tell me that?" Colton said he had no idea. "Probably because it's such an old name. Anyway, the table. I want you to have it. And stop right there if you're going to tell me no. I loved this table, but not the man who brought it to this house when we were married. He was a mean man, didn't ever want to use this, and when it came time for him to be buried, I almost said to use it to make his casket. But then his granddaddy, the maker of the table, came to talk to me. He was right nice, let me tell you." He said that there are some very nice people in the world and that he was sitting with one of them. "You're a flirt. Does your stern mother know that?"

"She does, as a matter of fact. My brother, Levi, he's ten times worse than I am." They were laughing. "You said he came to see you. I'm assuming that he had a story about the table."

"I'm almost afraid to tell you about it. It was used as a birthing table when it was necessary. Even a few times, he told me, as a funeral casket stand." She got up to show him the hidden panel at the bottom of the seat. "See those names? It was like a Bible for him, he told me. All the births that happened, the deaths that were laid to rest, it's all there. And with that, I've kept up the tradition, so to speak. Lives and deaths, but not on this table. Those were his."

"What a tragic yet lovely story." She asked him what he did for a living. "I'm a Doctor of Psychology. I'm what some call a head doctor."

"Come with me, young man." She got up, and he realized then how little she was. Shorter than him by a couple of feet, as a matter of fact. They ended up in what he only assumed was her bedroom. The bedroom furniture there wasn't being sold either, she told him. Going to the little lady secretary, she handed him a photo.

Her hands were gnarled with arthritis. Liver marks, he'd heard them called, made her skin looked tanned because there were so many of them. But her nails were painted, and her hair was done up. The dress she had on was probably her Sunday best. He loved everything about Alma Spencer.

"That's my first husband, the mean bastard, his father, and the man who made your table." He looked at the faded photo and thought of the time they would have had to stand still for this. Then he noticed what they were seated on. "That's right, the table in the other room. The year of that picture is about eighteen ninety-three. We were married at nine-thirty."

"You can't be that old." She told him he was flirting again. "No, I'm not. I had you pegged for about seventy-five to mid-eighties. If you don't mind me asking, how old are you, Alma?"

"I'll be one hundred and seven on my next birthday." Pride was all over her face, and he wanted to hug her. "You go on now and have a seat there. Not on my bed, that's not proper like."

He couldn't help it, he fell in love with the elderly woman. They sat there for over an hour, and he knew that he was missing everything that he wanted to buy, but he got so much more than he'd ever dreamed possible. She told him stories about her life, the furniture in the house, and how she'd come to have a Model-T Ford in the back of her barn. The two of them even had a slice of pizza together before he wandered outside with her to watch the goings on, as she called them.

He was given the pictures of the table and a few more things that she had loved. He tried hard not to take things he thought might be family items, but she said they'd taken what they wanted. Colton bid on and won two of the boxes of stuff that he wanted, and managed to get her recipe box all written in her own hand. When the end of the day came they were still hanging out together, and he invited her to dinner with him and his brothers.

"You don't want an old woman having dinner with you." They all three said that they'd love to have her company. "Well, then, I'll do it. I want me a nice steak, and I'll pay."

Levi laughed. "A woman never pays when they're with a Stanton. And tonight we celebrate. I just got a house back home, and the perfect desk to go with it."

She went into the house and told them she had to settle up with the man. So when they were finished loading their things, even the table and chairs that he'd never gotten a price on, she joined them. It was going to be a fun night, probably the best he'd had in a very long time.

Dinner was just how he thought it would be—loud and fun. Alma proved to be just as much of a flirt as she accused him of being. When he asked her again what the table would cost him, she smiled and told him that he'd paid her more than double by just being with her today.

"Well, I thank you. But I think you're getting the short end of the stick. I was the one that was charmed by you. And having all the pictures you gave me is going to make my dining room looked better for them being there."

She thanked him, then the other two, for giving her a grand time. When they dropped her off at her home, making sure that she was inside all right with her grandson, who was staying with her, they went to the hotel. It had been a very good day, and they were excited to be moving onto the next home.

The phone ringing startled him awake at four thirty. He sat up in bed when he didn't know the voice of the man on the other end. But when he said that he was David Spencer, for the third time, he remembered he was the grandson of Alma.

"Grandma passed away tonight." His heart broke then, and Colton asked him if he needed him to come there. "No. The ambulance is on its way, and she died with a smile on her face. I got up to see to her and she was already gone. I checked on her all the time. She was pretty old, you know."

"Yes, she told me. One hundred and eight this year." David cried a little. "I'm so sorry that she's passed on. She was a wonderful lady."

David said that she was. And wondered if he could come by in the morning. "Grandma wrote you a note. She knew, I think. Hugged me extra tight last night, and told me what a good time she'd had with you and your brothers. You certainly did make her happy." He said he was glad. "If you don't mind coming by, she told me to make sure you got this before you left. And I was to tell you that she didn't die in her bed, but on the porch swing out front. I don't know why that would be important, but I promised her that I'd tell you that."

"Alma was watching the stars, wasn't she?" David said that she was, actually. "Good. She said that people my age don't do that often enough, and they miss a great deal."

"She surely did like you, Dr. Stanton. She really did."

After hanging up, he got up to get a shower. They were to meet at the restaurant for breakfast, then head on out. The things that they'd bought were on their way home, and the driver would be returning tonight. It was going to be a while before he bought himself anything so nice as his table.

His brothers went with him to the house. There were several cars there, but he was met outside by David. He handed him the pretty lavender envelope and sat down with him at the picnic table. David smiled when he sniffed it.

"She loved to smell pretty. Whenever I see or smell lavender from now on, I'll remember her. She was the greatest grandma — well, my great-great grandma. You go ahead and read it, then her attorney wants to speak to you briefly. It's not about the table, that is yours, but about his conversation with Grandma last night before you went to dinner."

Opening the envelope, several pictures fell out. He looked at them and knew that one of them was of her as a child. The other two, according to the back of them, were her mom and dad. There was one of a baby that had no name on it, but it was a recent picture. He could almost see her writing the letter, sitting at her desk with her pen and inkwell close by.

~~~

"My dearest friend, Colton. I had so much fun this evening with you that I knew that it was time. No one could be happier, you see, than the three of you made me tonight. I have been wanting to die for several weeks now; my poor old body is just exhausted. You give my boy David a hug for me, and tell him that he was my greatest creation. He'll

182

understand.

"I called my attorney before we left and made some arrangements that he'll talk to you about. He's a good man, if a little old. You treat him nicely, like I know you will. He has some things for you that I wish you and your brothers to have. Tell Levi that the desk is very sturdy, and that he can make love on it whenever he wishes.

"I love you, dear boy. You have given this old woman a purpose in her final hours. And I cannot thank you enough. Love, Alma Spencer."

"This is a very nice letter." Mr. Chap wiped his nose again. "That old woman could tear you apart one moment and give you the best hugs in the next. The part where she tells you that I'm old, and you should treat me right? She was like that with everyone until you did her wrong. You must have really impressed her, young man."

"I don't know what we did other than to hang out a little while and to have dinner together. I never meant for her to do anything. What did she do?" He told him. "I don't understand what you mean, she left me everything. What everything? And why would she do that?"

"I'm sure you don't have any idea who she might be, do you?" Colton said that he knew her name but that was all. "A. J. Spencer? Does that ring a bell?"

"Holy shit." They all turned to Levi. "She's the painter. The greatest primitive painter there ever was according to most. I've some of her pieces at home." Mr. Chap laughed, telling him she gave him her favorites. "I can't take that. Surely the family wanted them."

"Perhaps, but she didn't want to part with them to them.

She told me that there was someone out there that would appreciate them more than her family would. She knew that they'd just sell them off and take the money. Alma wanted you to have them. There are ten, total. They're being wrapped up to move for you now. You're a very lucky man." He said he was amazed that she'd do this. "It was just like her to do something like this."

The room was clearing out now that the family had come by. Albert didn't care for the rest of them, not like he did David or Alma. She was right in what she'd said to him. They would have sold it all off and been broke in no time. The table that young Colton had gotten was worth thousands, but that's all it would have been to them. Money. This man would treasure it, he could see that about him. Albert looked at Wyatt.

"She said that you were a surgeon that has only just purchased a house. Well, she left you some of her second husband's things. She said that you were eyeing her collection of old medical books; those are yours, as well as his instruments. Alma thought that a man like you could have fun with them in his new house. Also, all the patio furniture that is off her room, that belongs to you as well. I guess she caught you napping there yesterday." He nodded and smiled. "You're a good man, she told me, and I can see it. Yes, I can see that all of you are, and your mother must be very proud of you."

"She is." Albert looked at Colton. "I'm still upset that she wouldn't let me pay for the table. She knew that I wanted it, and could have gotten any price she wanted from me." He told him that she didn't need the money, but the friendship she did. "What else did she leave me, Mr. Chap?"

"Let me tell you something first. The house was going to be bulldozed in a few months. A farmer got the land and has no use for the house. You're to get the contents of it. There are nine rooms full of furniture, as well as things that you would need for it. Linens that are of the finest quality. The bedroom suite that she used as her own. There are also a few things upstairs, more paintings that she put aside. The desk, I'm afraid, is going to your brother, Levi. She, as you have read, had ideas for his use of it." They all laughed, but Albert shook his head as he continued. "Colton, she left you the contents of the house. You don't have to take it all, but whatever you leave will go with the house it's taken down."

"The contents of this house?" He nodded. "How much furniture are we talking about, Mr. Chap? I mean, I have a big house, but this one is much larger."

"Nine, like I said, such as her bedroom. There are more desks and chairs too. Things that her family didn't know about, or she supposed weren't able to get into. There is her jewelry collection as well. Not all of it is real, but enough that you could sell it should you want and make some money." Colton asked about the fees. "There are none. She made this happen as part of the table that you purchased yesterday. Oh, I nearly forgot, you need to pay for that. One dollar, if you please."

He stood up and pulled out his wallet. Even the man's wallet said humble and friendly.

"Thank you. I don't know what to say." Albert told Colton he'd said plenty when he'd talked to Alma. "She did too much for us, but you can bet that I'll take care of it all. I just can't believe this."

"You made her happy, and that, my dear boy, is more than anyone ever did for her. But I have a favor to ask of you." He told him anything, just as Alma said he would. "David—other than the hug you owe him, he'd like for you to help him out with one more thing. He wants to drive the Model-T just once before you take it. You will be taking it, won't you?"

Colton was still laughing when he left the house. Albert loved that he was going to get her things. Loved even more that her stingy family wasn't going to get any of it. Looking upward, he told Alma that he'd done as she asked, and told her that she was a good judge of character. He could not wait for Ray to find out about this. The letter to her went out in the morning post.

~~~

Ray put the final touches on the furniture that she was having photographed. If this guy continued to give her shit, she was going to fire him and do the work herself. She could do it too. She was taking her own advertising pictures before this guy knew that a camera pointed toward the thing you were shooting and not at himself.

"Ray, there's a letter for you." She glanced at her assistant and just gave him the look. "You have to sign for it. It has your name on it. From somewhere in West Virginia."

"That's family. Tell the man that I don't sign for things that are from my family." The guy came around the corner and told her if she didn't accept this, he'd not get paid. "How much will you make? I'll pay you."

"I can't do that either, ma'am. I would lose my job then." Christ, she hated people and their rules that didn't apply to her. Which in her way of thinking, none of them did. Signing her name to the paperwork, she took the envelope and threw it in the trash. Going back to her work, she finished the entire set before she finally fired the photographer.

"Because when I tell you to show up here at ten, that does not mean eleven-thirty. When I say the lighting is all wrong for what I want, you're supposed to say, how much lighting do you need? And then—"

"Then you will not get the pictures." She put out her hand and told him to give them to her. "No. You're not a nice person. And these belong to me."

"Did your company pay you to come here and work with me?" He nodded. "Then you've been paid for them, with my money. Fork the drive over or I'll put a fork in you and finish you off. I'm serious. I don't have time for your shit anymore today."

He started for the door and she just nodded at security. As soon as he handed over the drive, she picked up the phone and called his boss. Enough was enough.

"Margo, it's Ray of Ray's Furnishings. I would like to tell you about the run-in I had with the photographer you sent me today." After telling her everything that she'd had to put up with, she ended with telling her that he'd tried to refuse to hand over the pictures. "I'll have to probably reshoot the entire thing, because his way was apparently the only way that there is to shoot my catalog."

"I'm so sorry, Ray. You have no idea how many people have called me today about him. I'm so sorry." She asked why she'd send him to her if he was an obvious problem. "He's the only one we had today."

Hanging up on her, she knew she had to find a different

firm for the catalogs now. And when she was finished with that, she'd have to reset the furniture and do it herself. Fucking asses.

When she sat at her desk, she saw the envelope had been put on her blotter. Picking it up, she nearly threw it away again when she read who it was from. Albert Chap. Great grandma's attorney.

Taking a very deep breath then letting it out slowly, she opened the letter up. Before she could get it unfolded, her phone rang. Picking it up without looking, she answered with just her company name.

"Ray's Furnishings, how may I help you?" The caller demanded that she put Ray on the line, that it was her father. "I'm sorry, sir, Miss Ray has left for the day. May I take a message?"

"You tell her that her great-grandmother is finally dead, and she needs to get her ass home to see what a shamble she's made of my life. The old biddy couldn't have died years ago like a normal person. No, she had to outlive—"

"I'm sure you don't mean that." He asked her which part. "That your grandmother made a shamble of your life. Right? You also called her a biddy."

"She was an old biddy, and what business is that of yours? Never mind, I don't care. Just have Ray call me as soon as possible." He huffed. "She's gone and sold the farm too. To some farmer, of all things."

Ray hung up on her dad. It was that or get into a shouting match with him that she'd never win. Her dad, her father was the opposite of her in every way possible. Mostly because she tried to be nice and he never was. Returning to the letter, she read what Albert had to say.

"I'm so sorry, Rachel, but your great-grandmother passed in the night. She had dinner with some great friends, and then she came home and went to bed. She must have gotten up in the night because we found her in the swing out front with a blanket over her lap. I think she was at peace more in those few hours than she had been since you left home."

"I had to leave home, Grandma, and you knew it."

She sat there reading the rest of the letter telling her about the funeral that she probably wouldn't attend, as well as the ride that her little brother had in the car before it too was sold off. There was no family left for her to go home to anymore. Not one person but David, and even then, she'd not get him into trouble by going to see their parents. She was bad news, according to her family.

Picking up the phone, she called Albert, and they both cried as she listened to him telling her about Grandma's final days. "The auction went well, and I managed to get all the pieces out of the house that you wanted. The large bedstead is going to be delivered in a few days, as well as the plates from the kitchen. You should be getting her photos from the books too, all of them if I can find them. They'll be a little later coming. I wish you could have been here."

"Me too." She thought about it for a moment. "Dad called. He said that I had to come home. Do you know why?"

"Unless it's about David, I have no idea. He's been sent to that school that you and Alma found for him. You should be able to see him anytime you want there." She thought so too. But wouldn't. There was no telling what he might have heard about her, and she wasn't in the mood to explain herself to anyone again. Not ever.

"Can you find out for me? And send me the bill for anything that she might have incurred when she was alive." He said that he'd done that, but it wasn't much. "That's fine, Albert. Are you sticking around now that Grandma is gone? Or are you finally going to take that vacation?"

"Your father tried to hire me. I have no idea with what. He didn't own anything but the clothing that he wore. I don't even know if that was his or not." Grandma wasn't as rich as anyone thought she was. If it hadn't been for Ray paying the taxes and upkeep on the house, then she would never have been able to live out the last years of her life at home. "Honey, you should come and talk to them. Tell them what you've done to keep them in cash."

"No, I don't think so. But the things that Grandma and I set in place, they're all set up? They're not allowed in the accounts anymore?" He said he took care of that the moment he'd heard from David that she'd passed. "Good. Let them try and figure things out on their own. I'm not going to be there for them, not anymore. All right?"

"The funeral will be the day after tomorrow. I'm assuming you won't be here." She said no, her and Grandma had their own relationship taken care of. "She loved you, Ray-Ray. With all her heart."

"And I her."

She went home that night with a heavy heart. Her great great grandmother was gone, the only person in the world who understood her, or even tried to understand her. Her own parents were too busy being not happy to notice that she had become not just successful, but also a billionaire while they had shit. Laughing, she went to bed with a smile on her face.

"I love you, Grandma. So very much."

Chapter 13

Tess stretched her neck and tried not to think about how long she'd been on her feet today. The house was nearly completely painted, and she wanted to get the curtains hung before they went back to work on Monday. She was just about to go get a drink when Jules met her in the hallway.

They're all asleep." Laughing, she covered her mouth. Having three babies in the house made it hard to get any rest. "I think we should go to bed and finish this tomorrow. And if we don't, then we'll hire someone to do it."

"The brushes need to be cleaned up. Then there is the floor that —" He kissed her to silence. "I think we need to go to bed. I'm exhausted. There is no telling when one of them will wake the other two. I don't know about you, but I could use a good night's sleep or two."

The really funny part of them going to bed at six-thirty was that she knew that they'd be asleep in no time. Making love had become a thing of the past for right now. The girls needed them more than they thought they would. And while they had help, they hated to bother anyone when they just needed to rest.

The twins were very needy, and breaking them of the habit of wanting to be held all the time was hard on them. They would cry themselves to sleep sometimes, and it hurt Tess in ways that she didn't like. But they'd had it rough, so giving them a little extra in other things was all right, they told each other.

"I've talked to Mom." Jules moaned when his body hit the bed. "I don't remember this bed feeling this wonderful."

"What did you talk to your mom about?" She laid down too. "Oh yes, I think you might be right. When I had to get up at three this morning for Ruby, I wanted to crawl in her bed with her and hide. What were you saying?"

"We need another nanny." She nodded, but didn't really listen to him. "Starting tomorrow we have one."

"One what?" She drifted off and heard something and started to get up, but Jules said he had it. When she closed her eyes again, she nearly got up to pee but decided that if she wet the bed, she'd just buy a new one. It was just too good feeling right now.

When she woke again she was alone in the bed, and she felt better than she had in weeks. Getting up, she thought that Jules must have let her sleep in because the shower was dry and there weren't any wet towels hanging on the hook.

Strangely, she felt like she'd been run over the longer she was up and moving. Her muscles were tight and she kind of hurt a little. But going down to the kitchen, she found a new person in the kitchen feeding Ruby, and someone else feeding

Leanna.

"Hello." The cook told her that the mister had gone to work. "Work, on a Sunday? Why? Did something happen?"

"No, missus, it's Tuesday. You've been resting well, then? I'm going to fix you up something to eat. I bet you're starving." Tuesday? That couldn't be right. Tuesday was three days from now. Reaching out to Jules, he laughingly told her that it was indeed Tuesday.

You let me sleep for three days? He told her she was breeding. *You say that like that's an excuse. Honey, we had plans to get the house ready before the baby comes.*

Tess, I don't know if you're aware of this, but we have three babies in the house now. Getting ready for one more was actually a piece of cake. I take it you didn't hit the nursery on your way down to have lunch. She said she hadn't just as a plate of food was set in front of her. *You should make a trip up and look. Dad helped me, and we even followed the instructions on the bed. Which, amazingly enough, were easy to follow and glued to the bottom of the bed. Makes it easy to take apart too for later.*

You think that there will ever be a later? He said that he was sure of it. *I'm glad you are. I feel pretty good right now, but I have a feeling that it won't last.*

I don't know if you remember this or not, but I hired a new nanny. There are three of them to help out now. You have to work and so do I, and we can't do that exhausted all the time. And when I'm home or you, we'll take care of the children. I got some rest too, and it's incredible how much work I've gotten done. I don't regret taking the other two on, they're a joy. But we have the money, so we might as well help ourselves before we burn out. She agreed with him. *Good. Now, I want you to go and do something for yourself*

195

today. Just so you can be a woman without cares just one day a week. It'll make you all sexy and shit for me when I get home. She laughed with him. Christ, she loved this man.

She did feel pretty good, now that her muscles had gotten stretched out. She decided that she wanted to go on a run. And to do it by herself. Tess had not been on a good long run in years, and was sort of excited to go. But after stretching and getting dressed, she thought that she should just walk for now. She'd been out of shape for much too long to be running like an idiot.

Nearly to her in-law's house, she was ready to go into their house and beg for someone to take her home when the big semi pulled up in front of their home. Going to the door, she was not only surprised to see a woman driving, but also that she was so beautiful.

"I'm looking for a man by the name of Dr. Denny Stanton. He's supposed to guide me to another home." She asked where it was going from there. "To a Dr. C. Stanton. Then I'm going to a home of Dr. W. Stanton. Geez lady, is everyone here a doctor?"

"Not all. But I am one as well." When she didn't respond, Tess asked her if she could guide her there by riding with her. "We were expecting you, or someone, to come and bring these things to the house. I'm their sister-in-law. Tess Stanton."

"Sorry, I'm Hailey Whitehead. And sure, that would be great. There's another name on there, but I can't make it out. You know this guy? I'm assuming that he's another doctor." She told her that his name was Levi, and that he was an artist. "Figures. Are you ready?"

They didn't have far to go, and it was sort of fun for her to

196

get to ride in a semi. She'd never been in one before. Calling to Brayden to have some of the pack meet her at the houses, by the time they pulled up, there were at least a dozen men waiting to unload the truck for them.

It took them over three hours to unload the stuff at just Colton's home. She read each note on the piece and put it in the room that he wanted. She loved every section of it. And when they set up the dining room with the deacon's table, the benches were a perfect match. Hailey joined her a few minutes after the last piece of furniture was placed.

"I thought I was going to have to unload this. My dad was sort of vague." Tess asked her who her dad was. "Peter Whitehead. He owns the car shop on Ninth. Driving isn't my job, but he got himself into some trouble with a tranny and needed me to take over."

"Is he all right?" She said he had two broken fingers and a slipped disc. "Oh my. I hope he's doing all right. Wow, that's great that you could help him with this."

"Thanks. I was wondering if I was going to have to get the other stuff unloaded or are these guys going too? It certainly made it easier." She said that part of the pack, cougars, were going to meet them at the next house. "Great. I have no idea why he didn't tell me that it would need to be off loaded. But I have a few more pieces that I need to pick up tomorrow at the same house. He must have gotten a great deal."

"Colton always gets a good deal. I've never known a man that got as many deals as he does. But he needed to fill his house and knew just what he wanted." Tess didn't tell her that he got it because some elderly lady had taken a shine to him. "Are you ready to hit the next house?" As they made their way to Wyatt's house, she thought of the woman beside her. "You work on cars then?"

"Most of the time I'm a teacher. I used to teach kindergarten at a private school in Columbus. But funding fell through when the owners decided to not pay into our pensions and payrolls, and we were left without jobs. Sucks, but at least I can work for my dad, and he pays enough for me to eat and have clean underwear." She laughed with her. "I'm not usually so open with strangers. Oh hell, yes, I am. But I'm tired and I need some sleep. Then I have to go back out with this thing in the morning."

"You're doing pick up too?" She said that her dad was too hurt to drive. "I can see if we can send some of these guys with you. It might save on your own back too. And I know that they could use the work. The pack here, it's been down for a little while with work."

"If any of them know car repair, my dad has some openings. With the economy down like it is, people are keeping their cars a lot longer and making repairs rather than buying new." Tess said she could understand that. "I have an old beater, but Dad and I are working on a '66 Mustang convertible. It's not cherry yet, but it's getting there. It's really fun."

Talking with Brayden about the shop, he spoke to the wolf pack, and found four that could work at the repair shop. He was also able to arrange for a few of them to go with Hailey to the next few stops. There were only four along the route, and everything should fit in one load of the semi. Hailey was also invited to dinner with the family.

"I don't want to intrude. Dad said we could have pizza

tonight. That way I can get an early start in the morning. And neither one of us cook. I can microwave, but that's the extent of my abilities in the kitchen." Laughing, Tess told her to invite her dad as well. "You're serious? I'll call him and ask. But don't expect too much. He's not the visiting strangers type. You'd think the opposite the way he chats it up at the shop, but that's friends, he tells me. And people in need. My dad is wonderful, but he's a dork."

After a few minutes on the phone, Hailey said that he'd join them. And when they pulled in the yard at her in-laws, they were greeted by the rest of the family. It was nice, the way they just opened their home to people, Tess thought. And Hailey seemed to be a very nice person.

After dinner, Hailey's dad dozed in the chair while she and the other women sat out on the deck. It was getting warmer all the time, and she loved the outdoors. Even the babies seemed to be having a lot of fun, and Hailey helped out by feeding Julia her bottle.

"I used to live around here when I was younger. My parents split up when I was ten and I went with her, my brother with my dad. I haven't any idea why, but we didn't complain. It was fun going to the other house when we visited, and Grandma was around then." She burped the baby like a pro. "I have two nieces and some nephews. As well as two brothers, as well as a sister — much younger, all of them. Well, they're step-relations, but I love them. Anyway, you have a nice spread here."

"This is the best place. Quiet, but not too much. Not a lot of cars racing around. And then there is the added bonus of all of us being close together." She said she noticed that. "I love the stuff you picked up for Colton. It's perfect for him."

"I love the old too. Right now I'm working on stripping down a bread cabinet that was my grandmas. I don't have much room for it when I get it finished, so it'll probably end up in the bathroom with the tub, but I don't care. I love it."

They were laughing when Lucy came out and brought tea with her. "Honey, your dad is sound asleep, and I made up one of the rooms for you to sleep in tonight. There is no reason for you to go home only to have to come back in the morning for the truck." Hailey said it was fine, she didn't mind. "You mustn't argue with your elders, my dear. I'll see you ladies in the morning. Remember, we have to go and finish the bake sale at the shelter."

Hailey looked at her. "So, I guess I'm staying." They laughed, and it felt good. They all sat out on the porch until well after midnight before going in. Hailey stopped her at the door when she was leaving. "Thank you for today. I mean for everything. Talking to me, dinner, and friends. Thanks."

"It was my pleasure."

As she and Jules made their way home with the babies, Tess had a feeling that one of the boys, as Lucy called them, was about to get a mate. She asked Jules about his feelings on that.

"I was thinking the same thing. I think it'll be Levi because she's so neat and he's such a slob. Did you see the way she laid out everything to change a diaper? Everything right there where she could grab it. Levi would have had to make three trips to the diaper bag, and still would have put the diaper on backwards at least once." They both laughed. "I know that I've done the same thing. But I'm getting better."

"You are. And the fact that you can put a sleeper on them without cursing is an added bonus for them."

They entered the house and the nannies were waiting. While she loved her daughters very much, to have someone help like this, it was wonderful. Going to the living room, they sat down and watched some television. Yes, Tess thought, this could be wonderful.

~~~

Picking up the last pieces had been made much easier by the pack that had met her at each spot. The first group had been the biggest, as there was still a lot of furniture to get at the old house. Hailey noticed that there was a lot of heavy equipment on the land now and wondered aloud about that.

"The old woman there died a few days ago, and this farmer that has the next land over has purchased it. He's going to plow it up and plant corn and soy beans. Seems a shame, but then I heard that the house was too old to repair anyway." She nodded as some other pieces, not on her list, were being brought out. A very well-dressed lady, even though she was in jeans, seemed to be in charge. She also looked like she was waiting for someone to come out of the woods or up the drive to get her.

"Why don't we help her?" Barry, the wolf in charge of the help she had, said they could do that and went into the house to do so.

When a car came up the drive, she saw the other woman stiffen, and even from this distance, she could see that she was afraid. Walking toward her slowly, she told the woman her name.

"Ray Spencer. That man there, I'm afraid, is my father.

And as much as I'd love to punch him in the face, he's a fat fuck that'll hurt me." Hailey looked her up and down and said she thought she could take him. "I probably could, but he'd hurt my brother, David."

"Well, we can't have that." Hailey whistled as soon as the man got out of the car, and she felt rather than saw the pack come out of the house. The man at the car was a fat fucker. He had to weigh at least three hundred pounds. "Don't let him fall on you."

They were laughing when he came to stand in front of them, and Hailey was glad to see him pissed off about it. The pack moved closer and she felt better, but he wasn't going to hurt this woman. He shouldn't be hurting any woman, but especially not his grown daughter.

"Father. I thought you were told to stay away from me." She didn't stop staring at him and it seemed to unnerve him a bit. When he looked at her, Hailey wanted to hit him square in the fat face. "I'm here to get my things."

"Your things? You don't have shit here. Why aren't you at your little business and letting me go see what I can get? She gave it all away, did you hear that? Some stranger that bought her a dinner." Ray said that perhaps he was nice to her. "Nice? Like she'd been to me. My grandmother wasn't nice to anyone. Except you, I guess."

"Yes, well, I loved her. And she loved me. More than I can say for you, I guess."

Hailey saw him double up his fist and knew that he was going to hit her. While it wasn't any of her business, she didn't want the woman hurt. There was something about her, even with her strong words, that made Hailey think she was fragile.

"You should leave." He looked at Hailey fully finally. "She said there was some sort of order about you not coming around, and I think it would be very smart of you not to fuck around with that."

"You her dike friend? Figures she's get to the bottom of the crop." Hailey didn't care what her sexual orientation was, nor did she care if the woman fucked goats. But this was war, as far as she was concerned. The man had called her a bottom feeder. "Why don't you go and suck pussy someplace else? We're having a conversation that doesn't concern you."

Her fist was in his face before she could think what a bad idea that might have been. She wasn't going to live through this. But then she remembered the wolves when one of them sat on the fat man's chest when he fell.

Going to his head, she noticed right away that the wolf wasn't sitting on him so much as biting into his throat. That should get things going, she thought. Asking him if he could bite them both, a smallish wolf came to her and bit her hand as blood began to trickle down the neck of the fat fuck.

"Now, I don't know if you're aware of this or not, but the wolf currently cutting off your airway is a friend of mine. And since he's bitten you, he'll be able to find you at a moment's notice. He could also, and this might happen yet, tear your throat out if you don't fucking listen to me. Deal?"

He said fuck off. Benny laughed. *He's not very bright, is he? Also, you should know that he's armed. A gun at his hip that he can't get to without me tearing his arm off, and one in his boot.*

"Ray, your father is armed. Would you be so kind as to disarm him for me?" She did so and threw the second gun into the woods. One of the wolves brought it back. "They're afraid that a child will find it. But that was good to get it away from here."

"Can you understand him?" She told Ray that she could. "Good. Tell him that from now on, when he tries to touch me, come near me, or even to call me, I'm going to be armed as well. I'm finished with him. And tell him that—"

"He can hear you. But I'll translate, if I can do so word for word?" Ray laughed and said she wanted to hear what he had to say. "Good. He said that he'll be done with you when he's fucking ready, and that as soon as he finds David, he's going to fuck him up so that no one will know him."

"You touch him and I'll tear your throat out. And don't think I can't do it either." The man laughed. "Father, who do you think has been keeping Grandma in the money that you stole from her? How do you think she was able to live here all these years when you refused to help her with the taxes? Did you think that they'd just pay themselves? Or did you hope that she'd miss the payments so you could get the place for a song? Too late for that. I sold it to Mr. Green for a song, just so you'd not have it."

"You're a fucking liar. I'm thinking that he likes that word, just so you know. He says it a lot." They both laughed, and she saw that the pack had gone back to what they were doing, packing her semi as well as Ray's truck. Then it hit her. "Ray Spencer. Mother fuck balls, you're Ray of Ray's Furnishings. No wonder you could afford this place. You're one of the richest people in the world. Next—" She thought about the people that she'd just left. "Well fuck me. You're only exceeded by the Stanton family. And mighty Christ, they're wealthy."

"Yes, that's me. And thank you." Ray kicked her father in the ribs. "Don't you think it's sad that a stranger is not only nicer to me than you've ever been, but she knows more about me than you do? What do you think of that, Father dear? That your failure of a daughter isn't such a failure at all."

The police arrived about two minutes after Benny took off to the semi. They had all thrown a bag of clothing in the back, and she was glad now that they'd taken the precaution. Fat fuck was screaming about a wolf all the way to the cruiser. Hailey stood next to Ray while he was being read his rights and then taken away.

"They won't hold him long. These guys will help you get out of here." Ray thanked her but didn't move. "He's not going to give up, is he?"

"No, I'm afraid not. He might find David right now, but I'm working on that too." She asked her if he was safe. "Yes, when I can get him enrolled into military school. Not anyplace he wanted to go, but he would be safest there. Just have to get him in."

"I know of a place. A great school, and they have the best protection around. The wolf pack. There is also a pack of cougars. I can make a call for you. I don't know them well, but my dad can vouch for them. And apparently, your grandmother left one of them everything she owned."

"Colton Stanton." She looked at her. "You think they'd take him in? I'll pay whatever they want. I need him safe. He's all I have left after Grandma died." She said that she'd contact her now.

Going to her truck, it was arranged in minutes. Hailey

was to take him back home with her, in the truck. Until Ray was able to come and get him, he'd be put into one of the houses until other arrangements could be made. Hailey asked for them to watch over the woman too.

"We can do that. Are you safe?" She told Tess that she wasn't his target right now. "Not from what Dane found out."

"She was looking into my life? How sweet. Not really. Don't do that, and if you've already found out things, only believe about half of it." She said she didn't believe any of it. "Some of it is true. But not all. Anyway, if you could see your way into keeping her brother safe, as well as Ray, I'd appreciate it. And you might be able to get a discount on her stuff."

Making her way to the woman, she could see that she was going to be trouble. For some reason, she thought that might be fun for whoever was her target. But life, Hailey knew, was never pat, nor was it very good to someone like her.

Before You Go…

HELP AN AUTHOR

write a review

THANK YOU!

Share your voice and help guide other readers to these wonderful books. Even if it's only a line or two your reviews help readers discover the author's books so they can continue creating stories that you'll love. Login to your favorite retailer and leave a review. Thank you.

AWARD WINNING, BESTSELLING AUTHOR

Kathi Barton, winner of the Pinnacle Book Achievement award as well as a best-selling author on Amazon and All Romance books, lives in Nashport, Ohio with her husband Paul. When not creating new worlds and romance, Kathi and her husband enjoy camping and going to auctions. She can also be seen at county fairs with her husband who is an artist and potter.

Her muse, a cross between Jimmy Stewart and Hugh Jackman, brings her stories to life for her readers in a way that has them coming back time and again for more. Her favorite genre is paranormal romance with a great deal of spice. You can visit Kathi online and drop her an email if you'd like. She loves hearing from her fans. aaronskiss@gmail.com.

Follow Kathi on her blog: http://kathisbartonauthor.blogspot.com/